C000048236

The Woman who Swallowed
The Book of Kells

Ian Wild

To Leonora and Peter
Best Wishes

Ian Wild

x x x .

Published in 2000 by

Fish Publishing, Durrus, Bantry, Co. Cork, Ireland

fishpublishing@eircom.net

© Ian Wild 2000

The moral right of the author has been asserted.

ISBN   0 9523522 8 1

A catalogue record of this book is available from the British Library.

This book is sold subject to the condition that it shall not, by way of trade or otherwise, be lent, resold, hired out or otherwise circulated without the Publisher's prior consent in any form of binding or cover other than that in which it is published and without a similar condition including the condition being imposed on the subsequent purchaser.

Contents

for

B L P

with love

The Woman who Swallowed
The Book of Kells

The day that Freya swallowed the Book of Kells was quite eventful. Travelling back to Cork on Ianród Eireann, she'd had some difficulty concealing the fact that her stomach was sticking out at weird angles under the skin. She told an old man opposite that she was having a triangular baby. Talk about indigestion! When she belched, the air stank of old vellum. On reflection, she regretted hitting two security guards with a crowbar, but it was that or eating photographic facsimiles of the original. The taste wasn't the same.

Her oral fixation with religious texts started at the age of six when she had been made to eat Old Testament passages dealing with Sodom and Gomorra for saying *Shit*. Her parents had a talent for imaginative punishment that comes only with genuine religious fanaticism. Freya was twenty by the time she discovered, to her dismay, that other sinners thought eating bibles was *weird*. By then it was too late. She couldn't kick the habit and she had developed a connoisseur's palate where religious texts were concerned.

It's fashionable these days to blame the parents, but they were only doing their best. When every evening their daughter told them she was going upstairs to pray, they never thought for a moment that she was actually using these long hours of solitude to nibble at stolen religious tomes like an enormous

1

mouse at a block of cheese. Freya would lie on her bed and gnaw, eyes bloodshot, mouth foaming, until she got an almighty rush from this frenzied mastication. The only trouble was, the longer she went on, the rarer were the manuscripts she had to devour to get a buzz. One thing had led to another until......well, the Book of Kells had just seemed too mouth-watering to leave alone. Maybe it *was* an irreplaceable item of national heritage and of incalculable historical importance, but so was the potato, and people were always eating *those*.

When Freya arrived home from Dublin, her parents were arguing as usual. They hardly noticed her going upstairs, they were so busy throwing plates at each other. Once in the sanctuary of her room, Freya stripped off in front of the mirror. The book was taking a long time to digest. Her stomach still looked as if she'd swallowed a pyramid side on. She knew she would have to lie low for a few days until the whole coloured manuscript had travelled the long sausage of her intestines. No clothes she tried on could adequately hide the bulge. She would have to feign illness. If her parents got a close look at her abdomen, they would assume she was pregnant and probably have her kneecapped by the priest.

Freya was in bed when her parents finally looked in.

'You alright girl?' her dad asked, a huge shard of ceramic still sticking out of his head like a broken satellite dish.

'I've got a bit of a funny tummy.'

'It's all those beans you eat,' said her mother with the sympathy of a firing squad. *'There isn't a single line in the scriptures about eating baked beans. God's probably put a curse on your blasphemous stomach for not sticking to loaves and fish.'*

Her dad said:

'We just saw on the telly. Someone's stolen the Book

2

O'Kells from Trinity. Isn't that terrible?' He sneered: *'Yer mam thinks that God fancied a read, but when he put his big hand down to get it, he knocked the two security guards flat.'*

'I did not say that.'

'You did! How could ye explain it otherwise? Would it be Christian fer God to knock em on the head on purpose?'

'T'would if they were sinners.'

'Ah shut up woman.'

'I won't.'

'Ye will!'

Another argument began. Her parents went into their own room where there were more painful objects to throw. Dad's fist came through the wall.

'Missed,' jeered her mother's distant voice.

But the dysfunctions of Freya's family life faded beside the peculiar sensations caused by the religious toxicity of the Book of Kells. As Freya lay on her bed and stared at the ceiling, a hand holding a quill appeared and wrote: *initium.* The red word looked like it was drawn in blood. In fact drips of red seemed to appear across the plaster. Feeling distinctly unwell, Freya hiccuped. And heard voices in her stomach. The ceilings and walls became a golden blaze of orpiment, and funny dogs wriggled like snakes on the carpet. Then fish started to swim towards her over the bedspread. *Fish!* In early Christendom the fish was a symbol for Christ! It was time to crawl to the bathroom.

Fortunately, the argument between her parents was still raging, though now in Gaelic. Shooing half a dozen peacocks out of the bath, Freya locked the door and sat on the toilet. It was vital that she kept calm. She'd heard religion was the opium of the masses, but this was ridiculous. She picked up the RTE guide from where her father had dropped it. Even this

3

was transmogrified. It was all in Latin. Gay Byrne looked all flat with feet stuck out at right angles. The text was in dense black calligraphy. Then Freya heard angry screaming from inside the toilet. She'd started to poo little brown monks!

The drenched scribes chased her from the bathroom, shouting at the top of their squeaky voices, shaking fists at her that clenched miniature goose quills. No wonder her innards felt relieved. On the landing, Freya met her mother, who seemed to have lost a dimension and walked like Captain Pugwash.

'Mam! You've got a halo!'

Invisible angels sang in an eerie choir. Mam was too busy calling the last shots of her argument. She threw a copper pot into the bedroom. Freya heard it reverberate like a gong as it hit her father's head. Everybody seemed to be speaking an ancient dialect, and Freya could understand every word:

'Take that you oaf!'

She turned to her daughter.

'What are all these smelly little scribes doing all over the place?'

Then she noticed her daughter's belly.

'My God! You're pregnant!'

A posse of Lilliputian monks grabbed Freya's ankles.

'She's not with child!'

'She's with book!'

'She's a heathen!'

'She's swallowed a deluxe edition of the gospels!'

'She's swallowed the Book of Kells!'

Dad staggered like a cardboard cut-out onto the landing, still dazed from contact with the copper bowl. Both parents looked at their daughter's belly with horror. Aghast that their own daughter would be going to Hell.

4

'Freya!'

'You?'

The mammy fainted. Dad's two-dimensional halo went rapidly up and down above him, like an indecisive flying saucer trying to land. Kicking away the monks who were stabbing her shins with quills, Freya ran. Fortunately, her dad could only pursue her sideways.

Once she was out of the house Freya walked quickly down to the city centre. Everything seemed normal for a Friday evening, except for the calligraphy street signs and restaurants advertising specials of wild boar. A breath of fresh air was probably all she needed. It was merely a question of staying out until the effects of the swallowing wore off. Freya wished she'd never touched the stupid book. Maybe if she ate some kind of antidote it would help? A tabloid newspaper – *The Sun* or something. Maybe if she could make herself sick, the visions would pass? She stopped at Patrick's Bridge to stick her fingers down her throat, when she noticed something which made her forget all about prodding her tonsils – Viking longboats were sailing up the River Lee!

There must have been twenty of them, rowing up from Cork harbour. People congregated on the bridge to watch.

'Is this part of the Arts Festival?' somebody asked.

'Stupid waste of Corporation money! Think how much it cost to make them boats and costumes, and hire all them actors for the night. And there's people homeless on the streets. Still, it is very authentic. They look fierce. Are they real bows and arrows they're......urrghh!'

The man fell over, a feathered shaft in his chest. The crowd started to scream and panic as huge blonde-haired warriors bearing axes surged up the riverside steps and hacked at astonished tourists.

5

Freya legged it down Patrick Street. Behind her, Vikings roared and smashed Easons' front windows. Crowds ran past her, wailing, panicking, bleeding. From behind a telephone kiosk, she watched *Abrakebabra* being looted, ravenous Vikings emerging with huge hunks of meat on a spit. Hundreds were dead and dismembered before Gards in squad cars burst along Patrick Street. They'd barely stopped when axed windscreens burst like iced ponds. Further down the road, the invaders were pillaging *Argos*. Vast muscular Norsemen came out loaded with colour TVs and Hi-fis.

A distraught Freya ran home. She kept looking over her shoulder, knowing in her gut that the Vikings had come for *her*. She needed protection, but the authorities would be appalled by what she had done. They'd give her life and get doctors to remove the book's remains by caesarean.

Freya ran along her street. The front door of her house had been kicked off its hinges. Inside, the living room was wrecked. The telly screen looked like a newsreader had staged a breakout. But all the glass was *inside*. Religious icons had been yanked off the walls and snapped. In the middle of the carpet, the two-dimensional figures of her parents had been ripped to bits. Blood stained the floor like ink.

'Mammy? What happened?' said Freya, holding the disembodied head of her mother.

Throughout the house tiny scribes had been squashed underfoot like turds.

In shock, Freya staggered up to her room, where on so many evenings she had secretly eaten psalms, hymnbooks, and tasty bits of Genesis. Her stomach was no longer angular and fat. It seemed the book had been absorbed, and had become part of her. A low, deathly choir was still faintly hanging on somewhere in the attic perhaps, but little men tugging each other's beards had vanished from the wallpaper. Crying blindly, Freya opened the door of her room and stumbled towards her bed. She knelt beside it, hands clenched in prayer. But a word lodged in her throat like a sharp bone. She could not utter the word: *Christ.*

From downstairs, guttural voices shouted: *'Freya! Freya!'*

She leapt over her bed, flattening herself against a wall. They had come for her! Expecting to be murdered or raped, she shrieked as a band of filthy Vikings entered her room and roared in triumph, raising their bloodied axes to the roof. But unexpectedly, the winged helmets bowed. On their knees, the pagans announced that she was their Goddess.

A few hours later, looking over the side of a longboat, with a heap of plundered washing machines, microwaves and exercise bikes nearby, Freya watched the sun set on a calm sea. Her warriors rowed, their bare muscles glistening with sweat. In Nordic song, they were creating the saga of Freya: *The Woman Who Swallowed The Book Of Kells.* It all seemed so inevitable. So right. And though Freya stared long and deep into the darkening waters, she didn't see one single fish.

Garcia's Moustache

'It's a moustache in a million Garcia. Please, for your old mother's sake, don't shave it off.'

Garcia stroked the luxuriant hair on his upper lip with the air of an executioner. Curling mischievously at the ends, it was a moustache to drive women mad. Even women who detested moustaches had only to see Garcia across a room to be transfixed – then overcome by a desire to be kissed by him. But the kiss, often passionate on a balcony, grand piano, or even in a wardrobe, always went wrong. At the moment of consummation, as lips met, the moustache would go haywire. Stand on end. Try to climb up the woman's nostrils. Emit a crackle of static electricity, which would send rich and beautiful women screaming, trembling, horrified to the other side of the room, hands protecting their molested lips. The previous night, Garcia had kissed his latest model – Julia – by the riverside and his facial hair had gone wild. Rippling up her cheeks and tickling her ears. She had stepped backwards in shock. Then toppled into the river, shattering reflections of the city lights with an almighty splash. Garcia leapt to her rescue, but Julia swam away from him yelling for the police.

'It's nothing but trouble mother.'

Garcia held a razor, shaving foam, after-shave.

'But you look so handsome with the moustache. Just like your father.'

Of course Garcia Lopez was not his real name. His real name was Eric Broadbottom. But he knew he would never succeed in the art world with such a plebeian appendage. Nor was the old woman his mother. She was an out of work actress he had taken in to mind the shop whilst he worked. She was part of the image he had grown. So was the moustache. Garcia knew sales of his fantastical paintings would slow if people stopped seeing him as a toreador of the visual arts, stabbing gory paintbrushes into canvas as if at the kill. But for his emotional life to progress, he had to get past the first kiss with a woman.

'Go back up to the shop mother. I think I hear customers rustling their money.'

Garcia looked in the bathroom mirror at his handsome face and said aloud:

'To be great an artist must make sacrifices'

He massaged a blob of shaving foam onto his bristling lip. Then took up the razor and, stretching his face with the air of a master shaver, prepared for the first cut. Ole......! Somehow he had missed. The crowd in his mind booed. With greater resolve he went for another pass. Ole......! This time he could have sworn the moustache had shifted. Impossible. Surely, moustaches don't move? Not even Salvador Dali's. He would have to scrape the thing off with a toreador's flourish – right across the top lip. Ole......! This last time there was no doubt. The moustache dodged the razor – scuttling up Garcia's face with the agility of a cornered rat......A chase began, round and round his face went the fugitive moustache and slashing razor. Garcia was bleeding everywhere, but not a bristle had been cut.

Covered in sticking plasters Garcia went back to his studio.

'Ah! So you kept it after all, my boy.' His mother kissed

Band-Aid. *'And I have sold another painting. To a Miss Benjamin. She wants very much to meet you.'*

Lucy Benjamin was puzzled. Men were normally crazy to kiss her. Sometimes she even let them. But whenever she drew close to Garcia in restaurants and angled her face up – lips trembling and rouged – he shuddered and had to be excused. It took all her self-control not to grab his lapels and violently prise open his mouth with her tongue. She would have got more action from a shop window dummy. Obsessed with seducing Garcia, she asked, in her fat chequebook voice, if he would like a holiday in Paris, a weekend that she hoped would make swamp wrestling look hygienic.

It all happened in the Louvre.

'Ah Garcia!' said his mother as he packed, *'You've been together two weeks. So much longer than the others. She's a good girl. She won't make you happy. But she'll make you rich. And that's better than a kick in the jacks. And don't forget to kiss her in the Louvre. Where your father first kissed me.'*

Garcia had no intention of kissing Lucy in the Louvre. But as Lucy wriggled through a crowd to see the Mona Lisa, dragging Garcia into reluctantly parting tourists, there was a scream.

'She's wearing a moustache!'

An American cried out.

'Hey! Move over guys. Somebody's fainted.'

'Stop shoving!'

' Are you sure this isn't the one by Marcel Duchamps?'

Scandalised connoisseurs threw Garcia to one side. But not before he glimpsed the dimly lit masterpiece. Garcia's hand shot to his top lip. Mona was wearing **his** moustache!

A curator hurried to unlock the picture's glass surround. Security guards held the crowd at bay. There were more screams as the moustache shot over the curator's shoulders like a scalded ferret and escaped.

'It's alive!'

Tourists scattered in panic. Security guards scrabbled frantically as they tried to arrest the high-speed hairpiece. But Garcia was staring at Lucy.

'Lucy,' he said from behind his programme. *'Close your eyes. I want to kiss you.'*

'What? Now?'

'Just close them!'

Amidst mass hysteria, as the moustache slid across the ceiling, Lucy shut her long long lashes and smiled. Garcia took her in his arms. All around him people were shrieking and writhing. But at the moment of drawing towards Lucy's face, there was a strange furry sensation up Garcia's trouser leg. Something bristly shot through his underpants and up his torso. The moustache slipped into place on his top lip and he pulled away.

'For God's sake Garcia!!!!!'

Lucy grabbed his head and gave him a nose-flattening kiss.

The moustache didn't even twitch.

Wondering if he could at last kiss to his heart's content, the painter got carried away. Years of passion surged through him. Lucy's eyes bulged. Her legs lifted of the ground and curled about his middle. People went silent and stared. There was a gasp.

'Garcia!'

'Lucy!'

They were prized apart by the museum curator.

'Monsieur! Madame!'

'Ow!' Garcia exclaimed as the man gave his moustache an almighty tug.

'Pardon monsieur. Just checking. Now you must leave. And no more kissing. Just because you are in France, people think to make love anywhere. Go to a hotel. Now. Out.'

In the hotel room, Lucy ripped off Garcia's clothes. When down to his shirt and socks he thought he'd better confess.

'Lucy. I have to tell you something.'

Her fingers slowed on his shirt buttons.

'You've got something?'

'No.'

'You're married?'

'No.'

Buttons popped as she wrenched his shirt apart. He caught her hands:

'It's my......'

The moustache leapt off his face and down Lucy's front. She screamed, and contorted as the bristly creature sped around under her clothes.

'Garcia!'

Garcia grabbed where the moustache seemed to be. Lucy punched him in the mouth.

'Don't you molest me! Arrgggh! It's in my knickers!'

As Lucy struggled out of her underwear, the Hotel Manager knocked on the door. Carpeted, with a bloody mouth and broken tooth, Garcia saw the moustache fly down Lucy's leg and under the bed. The door was broken in by hotel staff.

'Monsieur! What is going on!'

'He's a pervert!' she spluttered.

*'Please! That is not important. There is a **hotel Inspector** downstairs...'*

The Manager fought to restrain an outraged Lucy.

'He's trained a rat to lie on his lip like a moustache.'

'Mon Dieu! Don't say that word, The Inspector!'

12

'He kissed me with a rat on his lip!'

'Mademoiselle! Shhh! There are no little furry things here. Look I pay you twenty thousand francs to hush this up.'

'There was a rat on his lip! A rat! A rat!'

Lucy writhed, hysterical in the grip of the Manager as a tall, forbidding man entered the room. He stared at the dishevelled tableau, eyes like spring onion bulbs.

'Monsieur! Est-ce que j'ai entendu le mot: RAT?'

Garcia looked for his underpants.

The manager hid Lucy behind him,

'Non, non,' he laughed feebly, *'she had a bad dream, woke up, saw a little grasshopper run across her husbands lip andæ...'*

Garcia winced as Lucy punched the manager who keeled into the arms of his staff, spluttering blood. For an elegant society woman she packed one hell of a punch. The Manager laughed weakly:

*'La madamoiselle est **Anglais**. Ils sont tous **madde**.'*

Garcia returned home *sans* Lucy and his mother arranged an appointment with a dentist for the broken tooth. In the waiting room Mrs Lopez tweaked Garcia's moustache.

'You drive him to celibacy! Behave when he meets another girl or he'll drop his image. Go back to being a six-stone weakling and painting in watercolours. Yes, then you will look stupid hanging on him. Like a fox's tail on a gerbil.'

'Mr Lopez?' said the receptionist. *'Miss Brosse will see you now.'*

Mrs Lopez crossed herself.

'Don't worry. Your father had all his teeth knocked out by Civil Guards in Seville. It saved him a lot of money, because they were all rotten. He wrote and thanked General Franco every week. I won't wait for you. I must go now and weep on

your father's grave.'

Garcia entered the surgery. Miss Brosse had her back to him, sterilising instruments.

'Just take a seat Mr Lopez.'

She turned to reveal a voluptuousness that made the word 'woman' seem an understatement. Sighting Garcia's moustache, she stiffened and came slowly towards him, entranced.

'Mr Lopez.'

His moustache twirled like an aeroplane propeller.

'Please...open your mouth...'

Garcia lay back, shut his eyes and then she was kissing him, fingers scrabbling for the intercom.

'Ahem Julie. Send the rest of the...er...clients home. And take the rest of the day off yourself. Mr Lopez's mouth needs a lot of filling. I mean fillings...'

She unzipped her white coat and stepped out of it

'Miss Brosse.'

'Emma,' she replied throwing underwear to dangle on an anglepoise drill.

'I am fascinated...' she said tearing off his trousers. *'By that indefinable quality of masculinity you have, something bristling and...and...Mr Lopez, there is something I must tell you......'*

'I can't wait!' Garcia gasped and proceeded to make love to her.

'Garcia,' she asked, seconds later, when it was all over.

'Yes.' he panted.

'Why do you make love with your hand on your mouth?'

For the rest of the day and much of the night, they remained on the padded chair, eventually falling asleep. It was not until the next morning that Garcia woke, and saw the moustache had struck. **She** was wearing it instead of **him**.

'Here boy,' he pleaded. 'Come to Garcy. Hop on daddy's lip.'

It didn't budge.

'Why are you doing this to me?'

Garcia tiptoed round the sleeping Emma, took the moustache gently in finger and thumb, and gave an almighty tug! She sat bolt upright and screeched. Garcia grovelled humbly, but the dentist just stared at him.

'Garcia! Where's your moustache?'

'You're wearing it,' he sobbed.

Slowly, she felt the bristles and then inexplicably...started to **laugh**. Curling up in agonies of mirth.

'Emma! I know it's a big shock. But I can't control it...I......why are you laughing?'

'I tried to say last night, but you wouldn't let me...'

'What?'

'Well your face. Haven't you felt it?'

Mystified, Garcia felt his chin. He had a beard. Of loose black crinkly hair.

'You see,' giggled Emma, 'I always have trouble with men because......' She threw back the sheet. Garcia yelped. She was bald where last night there had been a luxuriant triangle of black hair. '...my naughty hair, it escapes......'

The Horned Women of the
Infinite Blue Rooms

The House of the Infinite Blue Rooms was rumoured to contain all that a man could desire. For this reason, it was said, no man who entered the house ever returned.

One evening, a nail-varnished finger pushed the portico bell of the house. After a long silence the front door opened to reveal a woman dressed entirely in blue. Two spiral ram's horns crowned her brow.

'Come in.'

The visitor seemed taken aback, but crossed the threshold into a huge blue room. Several more horned women stood up.

'You must be Veronica?' one said. *'You phoned about the house.'*

'Yes.' The visitor smiled shakily. *'I wondered if you might like to use our services. Veronica's Estate Agency is renowned internationally. We have offices all over the world.'*

The women looked troubled. The one who had opened the door took Veronica's hand, and led her into the room.

'We have defaulted on our mortgage. The house is to be repossessed. We're all very upset, because of our emotional attachment to the place.'

'Of course,' said the estate agent. *'I'm sorry if I've been insensitive.'*

There were eight women in the room and all were crying.

Glassy tears were sliding down blue cheeks as they embraced each other for comfort.

'Pardon us,' said the first woman. 'Let me introduce you: This is Hermione. And so is this.'

Another woman looking passionately vulnerable with tears spoke:

'I am Hermione as well.'

'And me,' said another.

'And me.'

Each woman spoke with full lips, looking deep into Veronica's eyes, as if terribly hurt.

'We're all too, too sad,' said the first Hermione. 'Perhaps a dance would cheer everyone up? Then we can get down to business.'

At this, the octet of Hermiones brightened. One reached down to an ancient gramophone and placed the big needle onto a record. A crackling waltz began.

'Let me find you a partner.'

A Hermione led the visitor to a large wardrobe and opened it. Inside was a male dummy in a dress suit. The Hermione laughed.

'Don't worry. It's only a stuffed man. They never get out you know.'

Veronica clasped this object of taxidermy and watched as the Hermiones began to three step around the room with stiff partners. After a moment of reluctance, the visitor joined in, smiling dutifully into her partner's glass eyes. Then the needle of the gramophone got stuck and the dance stopped. Irritably, the Hermiones let eight effigies thud onto the carpet. Then they crowded round Veronica.

'You dance wonderfully well. You've learned to lead the man, like ourselves. It's so much easier with dead ones isn't *it? They don't look down your front and try to undress you with their eyes.'*

'Let's show Veronica some of the other rooms.'

'We've all taken a liking to you. I can feel it. Shall we let Veronica be the one to sell our house?'

There was a clamour of assent as the women led her down a blue corridor into a candlelit dining-room. More beautiful horned women were seated at a long table where a roast meal was steaming. Veronica was introduced to more Hermiones.

'I love the scent of blue roses, don't you?' asked one, drinking the perfume of fresh roses in a bowl.

'I presume you have brought a tape measure with you to measure the rooms?' another enquired.

'In my handbag,' said Veronica

'It will probably take some years to measure everything. As you are probably aware, the house is infinite. We sleep in different rooms every night. But if we are to get the best price, we simply must have a proper inventory.'

'I was hoping to make a brief initial sketch of the likely contents of the house and then return with some of my girls later,' said Veronica.

There was a silence.

'That would never do,' the Hermione looked vexed. *'The thing must be done discreetly. One woman feels too many for some of us.'*

At this point, with agonised cries, several Hermiones wrenched themselves from the table and fled the room sobbing:

'No! No! She mustn't! She mustn't!'

Veronica shifted uncomfortably.

'...and in our present financial position, the sale must go forward as soon as possible. Please do not mention leaving

again, until you have completed your appraisal of the house contents, furnishings included.'

Several more Hermiones wept heartrending tears into roses.

'I've pricked my hand on a thorn,' said one, her bottom lip quivering as blood in one voluptuous blue drop went slowly over her palm like ink.

Veronica apologised profusely and swallowed hard.

'Might I ask the whereabouts of the nearest washroom?' she enquired when the meal was over. She was shown to a large blue door.

'In here.' a Hermione said, staring at her with troubled eyes.

Veronica went inside. There was no lock on the door. She lifted the toilet seat. Then replaced it, looking hastily round. She pulled down her underwear and took out a mobile phone.

*'Giles. This is Vernon...I **said**, this is **Vernon**...No. I've got to whisper. Listen. I've found you a house and it's going to blow your mind. It's got a few problems. Yeah...damp and a few other things. The House of the Infinite Blue Rooms...No, dinner's out of the question. I'll see you when I get out...'*

There was a tap at the bathroom door.

'Look I've got to go...'

The mobile was stuffed back in the handbag. Vernon was sweating with fear. There was no escape. No window. He couldn't remember how to get back to the front door. He couldn't keep up the pretence of being a woman for as long as it took to survey the house. It was infinite! Soon he'd betray himself. Leave a toilet seat up. Then he'd be stuffed by these beautiful monsters. But even worse was the name 'Hermione'. They were all named after the wife he had betrayed.

He flushed the toilet. Then went to the mirror to check his make-up. He had thought that dressing as a woman would guarantee his getting out of the house to make a fat percentage on the sale. But...the door opened. A Hermione came in. She stared as he smiled and went past her.

'Haven't we met somewhere before?'

Vernon stopped in his tracks. It was *the* Hermione.

'How tasteless of you Vernon. You're wearing *her* clothes.'

'Shhh. Hermione.'

He recognised her despite the curled horns and blue skin.

'I can't believe you left me for a woman who dressed in these.' She came towards him and lifted his dress. 'I suppose that's her underwear too.'

'Hermione. Please help me get out of here. Don't laugh.'

She pushed him out and shut the door in his face.

That night Vernon crept rustling from his four poster bed, and in a nightdress fumbled along dark corridors looking for a way out. As he tiptoed down three carpeted steps, a hand grasped his shoulder.

'What *are* you doing Veronica? You woke me. I always hear the *lightest* footfall in my sleep. The vibrations go right through me.'

'I'm upset,' gabbled Vernon. 'The immensity of the task is weighing on me. I couldn't sleep so I thought I'd do some measuring in the dark.'

Lips kissed his own.

'You silly darling. And without a measuring tape too.'

'I was just making rough estimates.'

'Of course. Let me take you back to your room. Which was it now? Three million and six? Or three million and seven?'

Another voice spoke.

'What's the matter?'

'It's poor Veronica. She's worried about the measuring. She's trying to do it in the dark.'

20

The second Hermione kissed Vernon and stroked his neck.
'Don't worry. We'll all help you.'
They led Vernon to his room and pulled covers over him.
'Go to sleep you dear thing.'

In the morning, Vernon woke to streaming sunlight. A window!
He leapt from his bed and looked out at an immense blue lake
surrounded by woodland.

'It's beautiful isn't it?' said a Hermione entering with a tray of
breakfast. Sun glanced from whorled horns in her orange-brown
hair. She gazed out the window with a sigh. *'I envy your having
to measure such glorious things. How will you write a
description of such a room? What poetry could do it justice?'*

'That is one of the rooms?' asked Vernon, barely able to
disguise his dismay.

*'Yes. Some of us are going to row across the lake with you
this morning to measure it.'*

In the room of the dark blue lake, five Hermiones walked
through high grass down to the shore. A longboat was tied to a
jetty. Vernon saw 'his' Hermione at the prow. She looked like a
figurehead. Vernon sat gingerly in the stern. The women
pushed off and set to work with long bladed oars, cutting the
still waters in harmony as they rowed across the lake.

'We're pulling a long measure behind us,' said Hermione
from the prow.

The others began to breathe heavily from their labours.
Sweat stuck hair to their glistening brows. He trailed his hand.

'Don't do that.' said one. *'Who knows what's down there.'*

'Two miles almost exactly.'
The longboat beached. A high waterfall gushed into a pool.

21

'Let's swim. It's so hot.'

'Come on Veronica. It's safe here.'

'No thank you. I can't swim.'

Two Hermiones grabbed his hands.

'We'll teach you. We'll all die if we don't get out of these hot clothes.'

'Really. I don't feel like swimming.'

'Alright then. Just watch.'

The five of them pulled long blue gowns off. With small screams, they slipped into the water. Shrill and laughing, they splashed each other. Vernon watched their blue-white bodies turn in the weeds. The blue of the skies, mountains and lake seemed oppressively dark. Then 'his' Hermione languorously heaved herself up the bank to sit beside him.

'What a lovely day.'

He stared at a healed bullet hole above her left breast.

'Listen Hermione, if they find out about me, will they...?'

'Like an olive,' she smiled.

The other Hermiones ran up the bank, giggling and wet.

'Please...' said Vernon.

'Don't worry. I won't tell them. Yet. Here, let me hold the other end of the tape measure.'

It was dark when the longboat returned across the lake. A bonfire was roaring on the shale near the jetty and more Hermiones were grouped around it. Columns of sparks fizzed upwards into the night as logs were cast onto the blaze. Vernon fell getting out of the boat.

'Come by the fire, to get dry,' said one of the women.

Tinted by orange flame, the Hermiones looked uncanny. Several were spread-eagled on the shore murmuring:

'Oh the stars! The stars!'

'Take off your shoes and dry them. Your tights are soaked,

you poor thing.'

A Hermione tried to unbutton Vernon's dress.

'No! Really! I don't mind! I like being soaked!'

'Don't be silly. We're all women too!'

'I can manage!' he said. *'I'll take off my shoes and tights. The rest is fine.'*

'You're teasing us. You'll catch a cold, silly girl.'

Vernon trembled as he raised his dress to the thigh and peeled down his tights. It was as if they knew. They were all staring.

'What divine legs.' said one, kneeling beside him, hand stroking his thigh. *'I love the smoothness of feminine muscularity.'*

She took her hand away and smiled. Vernon stood and placed his shoes and tights near the fire to steam.

'How on earth am I going to measure the ceiling of this room?' he asked nervously, looking up into the night.

'With rockets,' said 'his' Hermione. *'Rockets pulling a light measure behind them.'*

Almost as she spoke, there was a sputter and ripping of air. Rockets exploded spores of coloured light overhead. The lake was sprinkled with a million reflections. The Hermiones gazed up, clapping and turning underneath the display in ecstasy.

'Have any come down? How high is it? How high?'

'A whole mile and it still hasn't reached the top!'

The Hermiones shrieked as another round of fireworks burst aloft and spread a confetti of sparks. Vernon watched the women as they exclaimed and clung to one another in delight. He felt his disguise breaking. He could not keep up the pretence. Backing from the main group by the fire, he decided to drop out of sight and then run. Hopefully, they would never be able to track him down in this vast blue wilderness.

23

'There isn't an end to it! It's infinite! An infinite sky! Measureless to woman!'

Vernon was almost out of sight of the fire when he heard a Hermione cry out:

'Where's Veronica?' She was here a moment ago!'

Voices clamoured and before he could turn and run, a group of them spotted him. They came running down to the shore where he was standing. He began to cry.

'Oh Veronica darling!'

'Are you upset about the measurements?'

'Poor dear. She's shaking. She's freezing in these wet clothes. Take them off.'

'No, please!'

They lifted his dress.

'Come on. We'll warm you up. Don't fight.'

The dress was unbuttoned by laughing Hermiones. Vernon felt hands grasp up his thighs to pull at his underwear as the dress was pulled off. He shrieked. But another shout stopped the women.

*'Quick! Come quick! It's **men**! Men have walked into the house!'*

Vernon was left crouching by the water in his borrowed underwear, his dress clutched to his front. All but one of the Hermiones ran up the hillside.

'It's alright. It's me.' said Hermione. *'Get dressed and I'll take you to a room where you can get dry.'*

Vernon in another four-poster bed, was stark staring awake. Any moment he expected to hear far off screams as the men were murdered. Even in the cosiness of blankets and sheets he felt chilled. If only he could get back to the outside world.

24

The house had undreamed of potential. The blue lake room alone was worth billions. But he had hidden his mobile phone in the first bedroom. And he didn't know where that was...Then Vernon sat up in terror. His door was opening quietly.

'Who's that?'

'Me.' His Hermione lit a candle.

Relieved, Vernon said: *'Have they killed them yet?'*

'Not yet, no.'

'What do you want?'

'Just gloating.'

'What?'

'But you know, seeing you all helpless, curled up like a little child by the lake, almost made me feel sorry for you...'

'Hermione. Listen to me. The other women – they meant nothing. Much. Even Julia...'

Hermione snuffed the candle and left.

After breakfast the next morning, a single Hermione took Vernon to another blue door.

'Only one of you today?'

*'Yes. The rest are with the **men**. They want to buy the house.'*

The door opened into a wood. Shadows of foliage dappled the Hermione's face. The smell of greenery recently drenched by rain made the woman moan softly as she sniffed the air. Vernon followed her.

'Men are so repulsive. Don't you find them vile?' she asked.

'Extremely.' said Vernon.

'We all hate them. They are such an abhorrent shape. The sight of a naked man sickens me.' She started at sounds of laughter and men's voices nearby. Then looked confused. *'What are they doing in here?'*

There was a splash. More laughter. Through branches, a little way ahead, Vernon saw a man rise spluttering from flashes of water. The Hermione pulled Vernon behind a tree.

'Is that a river?' he whispered.

'Yes. It causes terrible damp problems on the rooms underneath.'

Looking carefully round the tree, Vernon saw women splashing the men in the shallows. Then they ran off giggling. Vernon saw a fat figure roaring with amusement and lust as he chased the blue horned Hermiones. It was **Giles**!

'Are you alright Veronica? You're looking very pale.'

As the group ran shrieking to another part of the wood, Vernon saw 'his' Hermione approaching, a posy drooping from her hands.

'Hello.' she said.

'We haven't started measuring yet,' said the other Hermione. *'I thought the men were going to be taken somewhere else?'*

'One of them just opened this door and ran in. They all wanted to follow.'

'I don't know if I'll be able to measure anything today,' said Vernon. *'I'm dizzy. Perhaps I could rest here for a while?'*

'I'll make a start, measuring the river,' said the first Hermione.

She walked off through the trees. Vernon and his first wife were alone.

'Don't try to warn Giles. That would disappoint us. The embalming fluids are all ready. Such exotic shades.'

Vernon trembled with panic.

'Hermione. You won't let them do it to me.'

'Why not. You're a man, aren't you?'

'Just because I ran off with Julia. I would have come back.

I swear I would. If you hadn't...'

'Shot myself.'

'Yes.'

'Through here.'

She opened her dress and exposed the dark hole above her breast. He turned his head aside. She came over to him. Took hold of his head and pressed it to the wound.

'Kiss! Kiss there! Where the bullet went in.'

He broke free, eyes large with horror.

'No! ...I swear I loved you. But...'

She looked at him pityingly:

'It's the wrong kind of hole.'

That evening, a Hermione led Vernon down spiral steps to a banqueting hall.

'Will the men be there? I don't want to see them. I hate men. Really. They're just terrible....'

She almost had to drag him along by the hand.

'You'll be safe from them, don't worry. They'll be gone tomorrow.'

She tugged him into a narrow hall draped with tapestries. A crackling log fire was at the furthest end. Over this, two boars roasted on spits.

'Let me introduce Veronica. She is selling the property on our behalf.'

Vernon did not dare look at Giles. But he smiled at the other men and curtseyed.

'And how did you fare this afternoon Veronica?'

'Not very well, I'm afraid. The river was very long, and we couldn't get to the end of it. It was rather beyond us.'

Giles leaned over towards Vernon.

'Haven't we met somewhere before?'

27

'I don't think so.'

'You're selling the house on behalf of these divine blue ladies?'

'They have bestowed that honour upon me,'

'How much.'

'I have yet to make a full appraisal of the contents.'

'But you must have an idea?'

A Hermione broke in.

'Are you and your friends interested in music Mr Giles?'

Some of the Hermiones were grouping at one end of the hall with mandolins and harps. The men, most of them chewing greasily, shouted approval. An octet of Hermiones began a sedate hymn. Almost like sleepwalkers, several men went over to crouch in front of them. Halfway through the second song, nearly all were gone from the long table. Giles spoke beneath the soft thrum of the harp.

'Vernon, why are you in drag?'

'Because no man gets out of here.'

'That's baloney. Besides, who'd want to.'

'Giles, don't blow my cover.'

'I want to buy.'

'There's no way. They'll kill you first.'

'Baloney.'

'Get the hell out. Before they spoon out your insides and stuff you.'

'These beautiful bitches?'

'Have you seen Hermione? **My** *Hermione?'*

'Yeah. So?'

'So this place isn't what it seems from the outside.'

Giles smirked.

'Think of all those Greenfield sites. Clean water. Unpolluted air. The infinite space for building, mining, construction. We're

billionaires so many times over, the dollar signs will never stop going round in our eyes. What'll they take for it?'

'They won't sell it to a man.'

'So that's why you dressed up.'

'No.'

'Don't get cute with me Vernon. 50/50. Or the ladies see under your dress.'

Giles rose and went over to where the Hermiones were playing and singing. Vernon stared swimmingly at the open fire where the roasted pigs had been carved bare. Blue tapestries swayed in the draughty hall. The women plucked instruments in a way that mesmerised the six black-suited men, and made Vernon feel faint and weak. The music was working on his nerves horribly. The women's voices cut into him like broken glass. He knew he would never sell the house, and Giles would never buy it. It was strange, but he felt he would rather kill Giles than let him have the keys. Vernon stood up and left the room. On the other side of the door, he began to regurgitate violently.

Vernon woke and lit a candle. Climbing from bed he stepped barefoot in a puddle. The ceiling was dripping. A cracked belly of plaster sagged above the doorway. The corridor outside was dim and he could hear no sound but water plinking water. Vernon walked for a while. Pools had collected here and there. Unusually, nobody was around. There were no doors. Just the corridor running interminably into the distance, and icy water underfoot. Vernon walked faster then began to run, hoping to find a door. But the corridor went on and on. He considered turning back. Then panicked. Perhaps the corridor was infinite. Infinite! He began to scrabble at the walls. Vernon screamed.

'Hermione! Hermione! Help me! There's no door! Where's the

29

door?'

Suddenly he saw one. Along the corridor a door was sucked open by a cold draught of air.

He walked into a cathedral nave. The sheer impossibility of the place astonished him. The arches seemed to defy perspective with their height and intricacy. Someone, somewhere was playing a mass. Down the rows of pews towards the altar, Vernon saw the distant figure of a Hermione, kneeling in prayer. Slowly and softly he approached and saw that the pews were lined with stuffed men in attitudes of prayer. Vernon found himself nodding with approval. What was this place doing to him? The organ stopped.

'Hermione?'

Vernon's voice echoed. She turned slowly and smiled, though tears glistened on her face.

'What are you doing here?' she asked.

'I don't know.'

He noticed she was drenched from kneeling in a pool of water. For the first time he realised that drips were falling from the vaults like rain.

'The house is rotten. It's crumbling away. We can't afford to mend it.'

'Sell part of it. To Giles.'

'And see him desecrate it. Him and other men. We'd rather it decomposed. As long as you're here we're hoping to hold off our debtors with the lie that it is about to be put on sale.'

'But the assets of this place. Even a fraction of the pure water...'

'It's poisoned.'

'The trees then....'

'They're rotten.'

'Hermione...'

30

He knelt beside her.

'Hermione. I'm scared. Please help me. Whatever I've done. Help me get out! I'm scared of this place. So scared.'

His jaw shuddered as her arms went around him. Then the cathedral was desecrated by a succession of unearthly screams.

At the far end of the aisle, where Vernon had entered only minutes earlier, the tiny figure of Giles was running towards them:

'Help! Help! Save me!'

A group of Hermiones were in pursuit – yelling with hatred. Giles ran up to Vernon and grabbed him.

'Save me. They stabbed the others! They're killers! Vernon! Vernon!'

The blood-splattered Hermiones closed. To Vernon's amazement, a herd of blue she-goats were bounding over pews with incredible agility, in front of the mob of women.

With another peircing scream, Giles ran to the altar. Two goats leapt up beside him. Finding he had nowhere left to run, he shook and fell to his knees. The women leapt onto the platform of the altar like beautiful athletes, their knives raised. Giles turned his back and was swiftly killed. The horned women dropped their knives and came slowly down from the platform towards Vernon. A goat stared at him from a pew. It shied as two dummies rolled from where they were seated and bumped onto the stone floor.

'Why did he call you Vernon?' one of the Hermiones asked, wiping sweaty hair from her brow, leaving a smudge of blood from her hand.

The other Hermiones looked suspiciously at him. He knew he was lost as they caught hold of him, undid his clothes. He shuddered at their bloody hands going over his skin and heard

31

only laughter as he fainted.

When Vernon woke, he was beside a fountain. Hermione was stroking his hair, and quaint, almost Venetian buildings shaded them from the sun.

'Hello.' she said.

'Where are they?'

He sat up and saw his reflection in the marble pool. He wore the velvet blue gown of the Hermiones. His head was crowned by two enormous curled horns.

'I saved you,' said Hermione.

She handed him a small object. Vernon held his own shrivelled genitalia on his palm: cold and calcified. Like pink coral. He was surprised how little he cared. He threw the object into the water.

'It was the only way I could get you out. Before the house falls apart.'

They were interrupted by singing. Both Hermione and Vernon sat up. From around a corner, the other Hermiones came dancing. They turned and bobbed with six stuffed men in black suits. Round and round they waltzed, until one approached Veronica with Giles.

'He'd like the next dance.'

Veronica rose, and unperturbed by her partner's blank stare began to dance.

'You see Giles, you are more likeable like this. So harmless and simple. And so am I.'

Giles stared emptily. It started to rain.

The stuffed dummies were dumped in the middle of the square and the women escaped over a small bridge into a blue door. To Veronica, as she left, it seemed the buildings were groaning and collapsing.

Near dawn the next day, Veronica woke to find Hermione standing by the bed. Gusts of wind blew her hair and nightdress. The room shook with catastrophic sounds.

'What's happening?' asked Veronica.

'You've got to go. Quickly. Follow me!'

Hermione ushered her from the room and ran down the drenched corridors. But Veronica ran in the opposite direction.

'Veronica! No!'

Veronica opened the first door she came to, and raced over sand dunes and wiry grasses. Hermione behind her screamed

'Veronica! Get out! It's breaking up!'

Veronica turned and waited, ankle deep in the last pushes of the waves. By the time Hermione caught up, it was too late. The sky was peeling off in dark blue strips and falling into the sea with tremendous splashes.

'It's caving in,' said Veronica. *'They will never have it.'*

They removed their nightdresses and threw them on the sand. Veronica saw the stuffed figure of Giles lying some way off down the beach. He wore trunks and sunglasses, and was reading a newspaper. Hermione was already in the waves, launching through them. Overhead, the sky was like damp wallpaper, peeling and tumbling into the waves. As Veronica reached Hermione, standing waist deep in water, she kissed where the bullet had gone through her heart. Miraculously, the wound healed. Then the sky plunged roaring around them, leaving darkness.

Leopold Bloom's Underpants

Ben Little was actually rather tall – over six foot, handsome and a lecturer at Cork University. Despite growing up on a crummy Mancunian estate, with a dipsomaniac dad, Ben had struggled through the education system to get a doctorate. In doing so he sprouted middle-class foliage to go with his working-class roots. It wasn't just that he got to like Keats and Shelley and other *Nancy* poets of the nineteenth century, he also developed a taste for posh girls floating about in Laura Ashley dresses. Ben wooed them with an odd mix of booze, football, radical politics and his own poetry, which eventually worked. Tamsin, a rich girl with a guilty conscience, fell for him at a Socialist Workers Party meeting and they were married in a month.

They moved over to a house in Montenotte when Ben got a job at UCC, and were happy as two people from completely different social hemispheres can be when they have small children. After an argument in which Ben tipped a box of cornflakes on Tamsin's head, he went down to *'Shaeffer's Antiques'* in Cork, to buy her a conciliatory gift: a Milo-De-Venus-type Grecian statuette with no arms, or floral china teapot. Shaeffer attended Ben's creative writing classes and could be relied upon for a discount.

'Looking for anything in particular?'

'A soothing present for Tamsin.'

Shaeffer chuckled.

'Pearl-handled duelling pistols?'

Ben grunted and went slowly round the shop. She'd possibly like the tiger skin. But it was politically incorrect. She'd definitely like the chaise-longue, but that was two grand.

'How much are the Gilbert and Sullivan books of sheet music?'

Shaeffer sucked air through his teeth and grimaced.

'Expensive. First editions.'

The lecturer sighed. His salary was quite large but so was his overdraft. Shaeffer held up some long johns:

'Leopold Bloom's Underpants?'

Joyce and Ulysses were a passion of Ben's. He caught a yellowing undergarment which the antique dealer tossed to him.

'Bloom's underpants?'

'You could wear them for her. But they're on the expensive side too.'

'These?' Ben dangled the long johns and snorted.

The antique dealer chuckled.

'Three hundred and fifty quid.'

*'You **are** joking. What've they got to do with Leopold Bloom?'*

Shaeffer held up his hands in a gesture of innocence.

*'I'm selling them for a friend. She **reckons** her grandad got them off Joyce in Zurich, who said they were Leopold Bloom's undies.'*

'Bollocks.'

'She seems to believe it. There's a letter goes with them.'

'From Joyce?'

'No. Her grandad.'

Shaeffer handed over a letter from his drawer:

'Dear Leontia, not much of an inheritance, I know. But

35

here are the famous long johns. Don't wear them yourself, even on a cold day! Joyce really did give these to me in Zurich, for procuring a little nightlife for him. One day they'll be worth a bob...'

Ben read thoughtfully. Long johns belonging to Joyce must be worth something. Especially if they threw light on his work.

'Where's this Leontia live?'

'Dublin. But she didn't want me giving out her address.'

'I just want to check the story. Academically speaking.'

Shaeffer shrugged:

'Well as it's you...'

He scribbled on a scrap of paper.

'Phone number?'

'Write.'

Three hundred and fifty quid! Ben paid by cheque.

Back in Montenotte, Ben tried the long johns for size. They were a tight fit, but think! They might not have been washed since Joyce had last worn them! He posed in front of the mirror and said:

'Mr Leopold Bloom ate with relish the inner organs of beasts and fowls.'

An adventurous excitement broke over him. Tamsin was fetching the kids from the childminder. He could catch a train and visit this Leontia. There might be an almighty academic scoop for the taking! Ben scrawled a note:

'Dear Tam. Poetry Ireland phoned. They want me to do a reading tonight! Somebody dropped out of a gig, so they asked me! Phone you later. Ben. Kisses to the pests. XXXXX'

He didn't want to tell her he'd paid three hundred and fifty quid for some undies. *Yet.* She'd think he'd been had. After pulling trousers over the long johns, Ben grabbed a copy of *Ulysses* and rushed from the house.

On the train, he emptied four miniature bottles of brandy and browsed the brothel scene for mention of Bloom's nether garments. He was convinced the undies would illuminate the writing of Ulysses. This Mrs Leontia, whoever she was, would undoubtedly know more.

At Houston Station he tipsily caught a taxi:

'Harrington Street please.'

As Dublin spun in a haze of lights, he imagined himself back at UCC a fêted academic detective, lecturing gobsmacked students – holding up the long johns as they laughed uproariously.

'Anywhere do?' asked the taxi driver.

As he'd expected, the flat looked quite smart. Ben pressed the bell, too sozzled to worry that he might seem a bit of a loony, appearing out of nowhere, asking some old bird about undies. A crackly woman's voice came over an intercom:

'Hello?'

She sounded surprised. In his best University voice Ben spoke into the plastic grille.

'Sorry to trouble you in the evening. I'm looking for Leontia. I'm a friend of Henry Shaeffer, an antique dealer in Cork. I'm a lecturer from UCC, up in Dublin doing some work. I thought I'd just drop by to ask about some long johns he said you'd given him to sell. I'm interested in James Joyce you see.'

After a pause, the voice said.

'Hang on.'

The door was opened by an attractive girl in her mid-twenties, wearing an extremely skimpy skirt. She was heavily made up and seemed embarrassed. Ben stammered as he introduced himself. Leontia smiled wanly and pushed back a mane of black hair.

'If you're a friend of Henry's you'd better come in.'

Ben walked down some steps into her flat, talking hurriedly to cover his confusion.

'You see, I lecture in Modern Literature and we're always under this heavy pressure to publish stuff. So when I found the long johns in Henry's shop, I just wondered if there was more to the story than your grandad put in the letter. It could be academic scoop, you see. That's why I bought them.'

She looked aghast.

'You bought them?'

'Yes.' Ben was puzzled. *'They were for sale weren't they?'*

The girl sat on a couch, biting her lip.

'Yes. Yes I wanted to sell them. I...just didn't expect to see the buyer. I didn't think an academic would get hold of them.'

Ben tried to ignore the shortness of her skirt and the longness of her legs.

'I don't quite follow.'

'Did Henry give you my address?'

'Yes.'

Her head sank into both hands with sigh. A dark curtain of hair fell to mask her face.

'Grandad was a bit of a spinner of tall tales, y'know? I'm not saying they aren't James Joyces'. Grandad always said he'd met him in Zurich whilst he was writing Ulysses, and that he got him a woman, and there'd been trouble and Joyce left his undies behind. It was just a tale. It could have been true. But he never told it the same way twice. When he died last year, he left them to me. I needed money. So I asked Henry if he'd sell them for me. He's a friend of Mum's.'

'Didn't your grandad leave any more details? Where in Zurich? When?'

'No. He probably would have done if it had been true. I'm sorry. It was silly of me to put them in the shop. I was desperate for cash. The rent on this place is mad and I owe weeks and weeks. I didn't think I'd have to look the buyer in the face and say they were genuine. So get Henry to give you the money back.'

Ben was hugely disappointed.

'Did he have any friends who could authenticate them? Who could give a little bit more substance to the story?'

She shook her head dismally.

'Would your Mum or Dad know more than he told you?'

'My Dad's dead. Mum and grandad hated each other. Anyway, me and my Mum aren't speaking. She's the reason I'm in this bloody mess.'

Ben sat beside her on the sofa, because her voice was going quiet like she was near to blubbing.

'Mum was paying for this place. She's rich. I'm a student. At Trinity. We had a big row a couple of months ago. I thought it would all blow over and she'd pick up the tabs, like she always has. But she just slams the phone down when she hears my voice. So...'

Leontia looked up, pushing back her hair. Her mascara was streaky, but she laughed.

'So, can you believe it, when you called just now, I was just about to go out down Leeson Street or somewhere and try to pick up a rich bloke for the night.'

She laughed again at the surprise on Ben's face.

'I read about it in the Irish Times. Students in Paris who pay their fees when they're stuck by......y'know............'

They looked into each other's eyes. Ben, inebriated,

couldn't stop himself:

'Well, I suppose, if you didn't go out, and you just stayed here...with me......we could call it quits about the three hundred and fifty......that is to say, Henry could still give you, y'know, the cheque.........'

She stared hard. Then slowly brought her arm up around Ben and pulled him on top of her.

What are a man and a woman in love? thought Ben as Bloom's long johns were pushed further and further down his loins, *but a cork and a bottle.*

At 6.am Ben woke suddenly. What had he done! Turned a poverty stricken student into a prostitute! Spent three hundred and fifty quid on her body and a pair of fraudulent undies! He was a respectable, married man with two children that he loved. Yet Leontia was snoring gently beside him. He hadn't phoned Tamsin last night. If he wasn't quick, she'd be onto *Poetry Ireland* and......! Ben got up and struggled into his shirt.

'Are you off?' asked Leontia, sleepily.

'Yes. I'm sorry. I'm really sorry. I was drunk. I didn't know what I was doing.'

'That's okay,' she said. *'Nicest three hundred and fifty quid I've ever earned. What does Zoe say in* Ulysses? *Earned on the flat of her back?'*

'It was ten shillings in those days,' mused Ben. *'You didn't say you were an English student.'*

From beneath a tangle of black hair she smiled as he put on a sock.

'There were lots of things I didn't say.'

'Like what?' Ben had the long johns up to his knees before he said. *'Sorry. These are yours again now, I suppose.'*

Leontia shook her head.

40

'Keep them as a souvenir. They're one of the things I should have told you about...What I didn't say last night, was that my grandad always said those long johns were cursed. He said Joyce had been wearing them when writing the brothel scene in Ulysses and whenever grandad put them on......'

Here Leontia threw back her head and laughed like a young witch.

'Well, he said some whore would always end up pulling them off!'

My Mother's Penis

It was only when she was on her deathbed that Mother revealed she had a penis. My sister Stephanie and I were sitting on chairs beside her, in a room darkened by drawn velvet curtains and the smell of unwashed flesh. In a hoarse whisper Mother told us of the terrible organ's existence.

'As you know my dears, your father was a very eminent psychiatrist. We had a mutual dislike of each other, which he claimed was due to penis envy on my part. So when he died I had his nether organ removed and preserved. Victoria, open the Ebony Cabinet.'

Her withered trembling hand held up a tiny key. Stephanie and I stared at it, then at each other. Even if Mother hadn't kept the cabinet locked, neither of us would have dared open it. We were forbidden even to dust the horrible black thing, and if she caught us so much as looking at it, she'd frown. So it was with a thrill of excitement that I unlocked the cupboard.

'There's nothing there.' I said peering at empty shelves.

I heard the fading caw of my mother's voice, then Stephanie said:

'The bottom shelf. She said it's on the bottom shelf, at the back.'

I knelt down and peered into the gloomy recesses of the cabinet. With my head almost touching the carpet, I glimpsed a bottle lying on two mounts, as if it housed a model ship. With

42

dread I took the bottle in my hands and went carefully to my Mother's bedside.

Stephanie paled as she stared at the bottle.

*'It **isn't** is it?'* she asked in disgust.

We both stared through the glass at a small object floating in brownish liquid. Having my father's pickled penis handed down as an heirloom rendered me speechless. Stephanie sat heavily on her chair and spoke with contempt:

'How could you Mother?'

I looked intently at the little shrivelled object, tipping it this way and that so that it moved like the bubble in a spirit level.

*'Who could be envious of **that**?'* I said, and tried to prise the cork out of the bottle's neck. But my mother sat bolt upright and screeched:

'No! Victoria!'

I almost dropped the bottle in shock. My mother collapsed back on her pillows coughing.

'I was only going to look,' I explained.

Mother's eyes were bulging and she strained to speak:

'Never...' She choked, *'**Never** open that bottle...Or......'* she gasped feebly. I gripped her hand.

*'Or **what** Mother...'* Stephanie asked.

'Or it will...it will......' her voice was fading: *'The **thing**....'*

'It will what...?'

But the strain of talking made her convulse, then lie still.

'I think she's dead,' I whispered. *'Mother...'*

'What was she going to say...?' asked Stephanie.

'How should I know?'

'If you hadn't started tugging at that cork, she might have told us. You as good as finished her off.'

'Don't be ridiculous,' I said.

Stephanie pulled the bottle out of my hands:

'I'm sure it's not Daddy's anyway,' she frowned, turning the bottle to get a better look at the organ inside: *'Daddy's was much bigger. I saw it once when I accidentally walked in on him as he got out of the bath.'*

'Pickling probably shrank it.' I said.

'Or maybe the hospital gave her the wrong one.'

'It hardly matters.' I said testily, *'We must telephone for a doctor.'*

It was half an hour before the doctor arrived. He was a small fussy man in later middle age, dressed in a black hat and coat. He examined Mother briefly, but soon saw how dead she was. I sniffled a bit into a handkerchief feeling it was expected. I had loved her in a way. Then I squeaked in alarm to see Stephanie push the *bottle* into the doctor's hand:

*'Might I ask for your opinion Dr Barclay, on **this**?'*

'Certainly.'

The man hooked a pair of spectacles round his ears and peered keenly through the glass.

'Stephanie!' I reproached her with fierce eyes, *'This is hardly the time or place...'*

I broke off as the doctor looked up in shock and, despite his wrinkled pallor, blushed:

'My goodness. It would appear to be......a......'

I coughed politely.

'Might I ask why on earth you have presented me with this....this....'

'I just wanted to know if all penises – or is it penii? – er, shrivel so alarming when preserved in spirits?' asked Stephanie. *'Is it normal?'*

'Normal?'

'It belonged to my mother you see.'

*'Your **mother**?'*

44

The man's eyebrows went up almost to his hairline.

'*The **bottle** did.*' I intervened, '*The actual organ was my father's.*'

'*I merely wanted to find out **for certain** that it was my father's.*' Stephanie persisted.

Dr Barclay looked from Stephanie to me and back again, his mouth open in confusion then gabbled:

'*But you surely know yourself. it must have been your fathers. Women have something quite different. Your mother would have had the same as yourself, er down there…*'

Stephanie looked at the doctor as if he was an imbecile.

'*I meant, I remember my father's penis being far **larger**.*'

'*You do?*' gasped the man.

My sister continued, oblivious of Dr Barclay's discomfort.

'*Oh yes. I saw him getting out of the bath once and it was colossal. I can't believe this little pathetic shrimp, this underfed maggot…*'

'*Stephanie!*' I scolded.

'*Well Father was a great man. Not given the recognition he should have got for his ground-breaking work in psychological circles on penis envy, but we should have some bigger memento than this. Do they wizen dramatically with age, or is it the spirits? That's all I want to know. You must be in your mid-fifties Dr Barclay. Is yours a bit more shrivelled than when you were say, twenty?*'

'*Stephanie!*' I almost yelled at her.

The doctor handed the bottle back to Stephanie with a ghastly smile.

'*You must excuse me. I have other patients.*'

He rushed out of the door, forgetting to take his hat and coat.

'*Stephanie. That was incredibly rude.*'

'He's supposed to be a doctor. Can't be much good if a discussion about penises sends him into a blind panic. What if you had a genital wart?'

'Don't be disgusting.'

'Or syphilis? Don't faint Dr Barclay, but I want to show you my sore willy.'

'I'm not talking to you if you're going to say revolting things. Give me the bottle, I'll put it back in the cupboard and lock it.'

'No. I want it on the mantelpiece.'

'Stephanie......'

'I'm going to put it on the mantelpiece until I find out if it **is** Daddy's.'

I usually ignored Stephanie when she got into this sort of mood, but I was too emotional after all that had happened. And I couldn't stand the thought of that *thing* in the bottle staring at me from the mantelpiece. Quite frankly, I was afraid of it. I tried to snatch it from her hands.

'It should be locked up.'

She dodged me and smiled her bitter, sisterly smile.

'Are you afraid people will accuse him of flashing or something if we have him up there where everyone can see? Or are you frightened that Mother will be exposed for what she really was? A crooked old bitch who did this to get her own back on daddy for his affairs? Put somebody else's really small dick in a bottle and say it was his. Who'd envy **that** eh?'

This last jibe exposed the fault lines of our family past. Stephanie had always been closer to my father. A proper daddy's girl. Whilst I always seemed to take Mother's side. I felt violently angry when she called Mother – dead only hours – a crooked old bitch, partly because it was true.

'If she'd wanted to avenge Father in such a petty way, she'd have kept it on show.' I said and lunged for Stephanie.

46

We fell over, snarling, and the bottle smashed against the wall.

We watched aghast as the glass shattered and preservative oozed over the floor.

'You idiot!' Stephanie shouted into my face.

But I wasn't listening, for the pickled object, liberated from its bottle prison, *moved.* It crawled slowly from amongst the splinters of glass like a revolting grub. Then turned to look at us: its revolting mouth *smiled.* I ended up with Stephanie on the other side of the room behind the sofa, where both of us shrieked ourselves blue and watched it *grow.*

The swelling took only a minute I suppose, but it seemed to happen in slow motion like some monstrous larvae metamorphosing in a nature film.

'Daddy!' Stephanie gasped, at a six-foot penis that eventually leaned against the living room wall, taller than Mother's 1920's lampstand. The eyeless worm looked at us.

'My fair daughters,' its mouth said smoochily, *'thank you sooooooo much.'*

Stephanie and I clung to each other in terror as the penis went on:

'Forgive me if I don't kiss your cheeks. It would be a little shocking under the circumstances. Now that I am free from a long and tiresome imprisonment, I can renew some old acquaintances.'

With a shuffling movement, it went to where the doctor's hat and coat hung beside the door. The mouth threw them up into the air and as they came down, the vast organ wriggled into the garments and grinned.

'Your hysteria at the sight of a male organ would have made your dear mother proud.'

With another cackle of laughter the penis swept out of the

door. Stephanie and I looked at each other, then I was sick over the chaise lounge. Hearing the front door slam, Stephanie went to the window.

'He...it's...flagging down a taxi.'

I vomited again.

'The taxi's driving off.'

I ran into the bathroom and screamed. The last thing I remember was my own hysterical face in the bathroom mirror. Then I blacked out.

I was stupefied and trembling when I came to. It was not until the next day that I calmed enough to talk to Stephanie about **It**.

'Perhaps we only dreamed it?' I suggested.

Stephanie shook her head.

'It was as real as you or I. But why did it run off?'

'To do violence to something or somebody,' I trembled.

'Not necessarily.'

'But the penis is violent by its very nature – a cruel organ with no empathy or sense of responsibility,' I said.

'Don't be absurd,' Stephanie snorted, *'There's nothing inherently violent about a man's genitals.'*

'There is,' I insisted. *'The act of penetration is wholly violent.'*

'Only to you Victoria. Or a nun.'

I flushed at her insult, but went on:

'Sex is a jarring poking experience. You poke a fire, or somebody in the eye. You can't make that kind of an action gentle.'

'You say that only because of the awful men you've been to bed with. That horrible Douglas.'

'He was only horrible in bed.'

*'Is it any wonder with a name like **Douglas**? If you chose*

48

men with better names – Raphael or Orlando – you'd find their willies more intent on exploration of mystery. Something quite harmlessly rousing.'

*'Well I'm sure **Daddy's** wasn't harmlessly rousing. Mother was always complaining that she hated sex with him.'*

*'He **was** called Alec.'*

The telephone rang and Stephanie answered it. After a brief conversation, she put the phone down, her face was yellow with alarm.

'What's happened?' I asked.

'Monica Edwards. Her husband is dead.'

'You mean Humphrey? Humphrey Edwards? How awful.'

'Yes.'

We stood face to face holding each other by the arms.

'Uncle Humph.' I bit my underlip in anxiety. *'Mother's only other man. But that was **after** father.'*

*'But they would have done it on her bed, you know, whilst **It** was in the ebony cabinet.'*

'Surely not,' I gasped, without conviction.

'It's just the sort of thing that mother would do. Make love loudly with another man, to rub it in whilst the...It.....was there.'

'Stephanie...I'm sure Humphs dying and what happened yesterday can't possibly be connected.'

'Monica says it was murder.'

*'**Murder?'** I choked.

'He was found dead in the bath, strangled. The police said the marks round his neck suggested it had been done by a large python.'

I clutched my sister in agony.

'Oh my God! Quickly! Telephone the police! We have to tell them.'

I picked up the receiver, but Stephanie snatched it from my hand.

'What are you going to tell them? That your father's six-foot penis has escaped from solitary confinement in a bottle and is riding round the city in taxis murdering everyone your dead mother ever slept with? They'll have you locked up in an asylum.'

I saw her point.

'Then what shall we do?'

*'She only **had** one lover,'* Stephanie pointed out.

'That we knew of.'

'Maybe if we get a new bottle and put it outside the door tonight, he...It'll...come back?'

'What if he comes back and...it's still the same size?'

'What's the biggest bottle we've got?'

'Maybe it will only avenge itself on one person?' I said hopefully. *'A sort of monogamous murderer.'*

'No penis is monogamous,' my sister said dryly.

For the next few days, I kept thinking I saw It everywhere. At Mother's funeral, as the coffin was lowered into the earth, I thought I saw a single periscopic foreskin peeping over a nearby tombstone.

Stephanie told me I was imagining things, but I'd definitely seen a tall figure in a black coat and hat, sloping off through the trees.

That night I slept badly, dreaming that I was High Priestess of an ancient Peruvian cult. My mother and I stood at the apex of a large pyramid and watched pitilessly as my father was dragged up thousands of steps towards us. He was screaming for mercy and I was sharpening a large knife. He was bound to a flat stone altar and mother lifted up his robes and shrieked.

'Chop it off!'

But when I looked between his legs I saw his penis was in fact a large cobra that bit my arm. I dropped the knife and my arm began to swell. I woke up sweating and gnawing at my own hand.

At breakfast Stephanie choked and sprayed tea all over the morning paper.

'Oh my God! Victoria! The Bleesons are dead!'

I dropped my fork. It rolled down my dress leaving a trail of egg yolk.

'They died in a car crash. Yesterday. After the funeral.'

'Father!' I yelped. *'Of course, the figure I saw was going in the direction of the car park.'*

She read aloud.

'The car came off the road and drove nearly a hundred yards over rough ground before dropping over a cliff. Though baffled by the behaviour of the driver police are not treating the deaths as suspicious.'

'Weren't they the ones who wouldn't visit because Father once poured custard on them from an upstairs window.'

'Only after they'd sent him a straitjacket for Christmas.'

'He'd tried to psychoanalyse their dog and sent it mad. It started biting everybody and had to be put down.'

'It was mad before Father put him in that padded kennel. He said the animal had human envy. Anyway, I thought pouring custard on them was funny.'

'Not boiling custard. They had terrible burns. Poor Fanny Bleeson couldn't eat puddings ever again.'

Stephanie shrugged,

*'Oh well. The police aren't treating it as suspicious. Maybe it **was** just an accident.'*

'Or maybe a...a...an...It............slithered up out of the boot and grabbed the wheel.'

There was worse to come. A week later a news bulletin reported that a group of eminent psychiatrists had been killed at a conference in London. I began to sob uncontrollably.

'It's just coincidence,' Stephanie said, stroking my hair.

'We've got to stop him,' I wailed, *'He's killing all his old enemies. All that anger he stored up in life. He wasn't able to let it out through the sexual act with Mother and now...'*

'But the sexual act isn't necessarily tied up with anger.'

'What's rape then? Why are colts, dogs, and bullocks castrated? To make them docile! Men aren't any different. After sex, men become tranquil and passive. Douglas always went to sleep'

I was shouting because Stephanie didn't seem to care.

'Look at you!' she laughed, *'you're angry now!'*

'I'm not!'

'You're just as angry as Mother used to be. But nobody's suggesting cutting off your private parts.'

'We simply have to go to the police,' I said, *'even if they laugh at us.'*

'They'll lock you up for taking the piss.' Stephanie warned. *'Policemen hate to think people are laughing at them.'*

Over the next few days, the gruesome details of what happened at the conference emerged. A police spokesman reported that thirty-two qualified psychiatrists had been brutally killed. They had been hurled against walls, crammed down the toilet, squashed into waste-paper bins. So much carnage that blood dripped through the ceiling into the room below. But relations between Stephanie and I imploded only when we heard that a solitary survivor was being treated in a psychiatric hospital after claiming that the murderer was a gigantic twenty-foot penis. The newspapers had a field day:

'Psychiatrist fantasises that mass murderer was a penis!'

'We have to go to the Police now,' I told Stephanie.

'I don't see why,' she replied, in an infuriatingly offhand manner.

'He may be a large part our father, but he...It!...has to be brought to justice. Before any more terrible outrages occur.'

My sister sighed:

'I don't know why you're getting so uptight about it all.'

'Uptight! **Uptight!***'*

'In case you hadn't noticed, you're almost leaping out of your corsets.'

I was baffled by her insouciance.

'Stephanie! He...It!...could strike again at any moment. And more innocent people will be strangled or bludgeoned to death. The very least we can do is go down to the police station and **try** *to explain. Even if they* **do** *laugh at us. We must help them work out where it is going to strike next.'*

Stephanie smiled so smugly I wanted to slap her.

'But I **already know** *where it will strike next,'* she said. *'Here.'*

She handed me a letter: *'It's from Mother's friend Gretzel.'*

'She's coming to stay.'

'Yes.'

'There's a Feminist Conference in town.'

'Yes.'

'Stephanie! How can you invite her here? Father hated her worse than anybody in the world.'

'Exactly, so when I found out she was going to be presiding

53

over **"The Relevance of the Electra Complex in the Next Millennium"** *I thought it would be perfect to invite her here and trap Father's prick. It's a delicious irony. Of course in the Electra Complex the girl subconsciously discovers she has no penis and blames the mother for her lack of equipment. And Father's major development was to show that girls, feeling they have been castrated, believe they will never hold power. I've been reading one of his essays this morning:'*

She opened a book that had been lying beside her on the settee.

'Unconsciously, the young girl comes to believe the penis is power. The key which is inserted into the doors of fecundity. Without it, a woman is nothing. Thus the woman who does not outgrow the Electra Complex wishes subconsciously to castrate men. The mother is blamed, but the man is seen as a tyrant subjecting women, when in fact females are actually being given a soft time at home looking after children. This fundamental misunderstanding at the heart of the Electra Complex has given rise to a generation of immature women rising to power on the back of feminism and women's liberation issues, leading to the collapse of modern morality and adequate child rearing.'

'What a load of ridiculous tripe,' I snorted.

'Yes, but it was these pages that Gretzel once ripped out of one of his books and tore up in front of his face.'

I was horrified that Stephanie couldn't see the irresponsibility of her invitation.

'It makes us complicit in a possible murder.'

'You do talk bosh Victoria, it's the only way to stop it murdering other people who crossed him in life. We've just got to make some kind of willy trap, that's all.'

'A willy trap? What nonsense you're talking!'

'A vast vagina with a cage door which snaps shut once it's inside.'

'Stephanie! You've gone barmy!'

'No, no! Listen to me. It's simple. We put lots of hair around the door of the spare room, where It would expect Gretzel to be sleeping. We sew and stuff crimson satin around the architrave of the opening to make them look vaginaesque. Make a pair of six-foot slinky knickers and throw them over the sofa so that when it comes in...'

'How are we going to explain a...a...big...you know – vaginal opening to the spare room to Gretzel?'

'We'll say we did it in her honour.'

'She'll think we're mad.'

'It doesn't matter so long as we catch It.'

I tried hard to think of objections. The idea was so indecorous and grotesque.

'When we've got it in the room, what do we do then? How do we get it back in a bottle?'

'We'll put bromide down on the carpet...' then, at my look of scepticism, *'unless you've any better ideas?'*

I hadn't. Reluctantly, I went to the shops with my sister to choose the correct shade of silk.

'What on earth have you done to the door of the guest room?' asked Gretzel when she arrived.

'Oh, just some things we didn't take down after Christmas.' Stephanie said uneasily.

*'Looks like my cunt **felt** after the twins were born. For God's sake, can't we take the stuff down?'*

Though in her late sixties Gretzel was still a *very* formidable lady. She stood in the jaws of the orifice with her hands on her hips, shaking her head.

'*We couldn't possibly take the decorations down yet.*' Stephanie babbled. '*They remind us of Mother's last days, and we want to keep her memory warm. Why don't you let us take your bags in to the attic room?*'

'*Hell no, that jerk, your father slept up there.*'

'*Well Mother's room then?*'

'*Are you kidding? She just died in there. It's kinda morbid.*'

'*Alright,*' I said, '*my room. You can have my room. I'll sleep in the attic.*'

'*Hey I don't want to throw you out of your room Vicky. Why don't I just sleep in the guestroom like I always did? Who cares if the door is a cunt?*'

And taking her bags from us, she walked straight into the guestroom.

'*No!*' Stephanie gabbled, '*you mustn't. It's…it's haunted.*'

Gretzel looked puzzled.

'*Since when? I slept in there twenty times and never saw a thing. Are you two okay? You look like you seen ghosts yourselves? I'd go to a hotel but I'm tired after the journey. So look don't bother yourselves about me. I can look after myself.*'

She sat on the bed and took off her shoes.

'*You can't sleep in here,*' Stephanie said desperately. '*The ghost of Father's penis haunts this room.*'

Gretzel laughed:

'*What does it do? Fuck the door?*'

She lay on the bed and took out a cigar:

'*You two are kind of nuts, but I like it. Say, did you ever see your old man's dick in that bottle your mother had?*'

'*Er…yes,*' I said.

'*We buried it,*' Stephanie lied. '*Are you sure you wouldn't be comfier in my bed with me?*' she squirmed in desperation.

56

Gretzel looked at her through clouds of smoke.

'You a dyke or something?'

'I just thought it would be warmer.'

'For God's sake. I'm an old girl. Let me smoke and sleep. I'll be outa here before you know it.'

We left her, sprawled on the bed, puffing at a Havana, then crept into Stephanie's room:

'Brilliant!' I fumed. *'Any more fabulous ideas Sister, for apprehending rampant......cocks!'*

Stephanie looked devastated.

'We'll have to move her. When she's asleep. Into Mother's room, and hope she doesn't wake up.'

'No,' I said firmly, *'no more of your hare-brained ideas.'*

*'We can't **tell** her. You know what she's like, she just won't believe it.'*

'We'll have to spend the night on the sofa outside the spare room. We'll get under some duvets and have some rope handy in case we have to restrain It.'

The next morning, I woke up to find Stephanie lying against me snoring. I ran to the spare room. Gretzel was gone.

'My God! He's got her!' I screamed.

Stephanie was awake and by my side in an instant.

'Search the house. See if there's any signs of a struggle or bloodstains,' she said.

I rushed into the kitchen to find a note on the breakfast table.

'Dear girls,

You looked so pretty camping out there on the sofa, I didn't have the heart to wake you and ask why you weren't in your rooms. If you were hoping for a peek at your father's ghostly member, you must have been disappointed. Thanks for the bed and the roof over my head. And thanks Stephanie for putting me in touch with the Women's Group in town. See you soon. Gretzel.'

By the time I'd finished reading the note, Stephanie was in the kitchen.

'You put Gretzel in touch with the Women's Group?' I asked.

'Yes.' She tried not to look defensive. *'I needed to get her here to catch the thing.'*

'But have you thought about all those women's lives you've put at risk?'

'If he'd come last night, they wouldn't have been at any risk at all.'

'He...It...didn't.'

Stephanie folded her arms coldly.

'If not them – some other people would have been his next victims. That's if he was responsible for any of these deaths at all. It's still only conjecture.'

'I'm phoning the police.'

I went into the next room and grabbed the phone. But Stephanie wrenched the line from its socket.

'No. We've got to catch It.'

'Why?'

'Because......because the police won't believe you anyhow.'

But I could see guilt all over her face:

'You want it for yourself, don't you?'

'Now you're being ridiculous,' she answered, but not meeting my eyes.

I threw the phone onto the floor and walked towards her:

'That's why you wanted to trap it here isn't it? And you're quite happy to endanger dozens of people's lives to get what you want.'

'Oh shut up Victoria.'

She turned away from me, hiding her face.

'Because it's you that's never achieved emotional detachment from Father. You have the Electra Complex. You want father's penis for yourself don't you?'

She started to cry.

'What the hell for, you nutcase?' I asked.

'I just wanted to go away with it. On my own. I thought I could make it happy.'

I turned Stephanie around and let her cry into my shoulder.

'Oh what are we going to do?' she sobbed. *'What shall we do? It'll kill them all.'*

'We'll have to drive into town and warn them,' I said drying her eyes with my handkerchief.

She looked at the clock. It was already nearly eleven.

'It might be too late,' she sniffled.

It was.

Before we even reached the town centre we could hear the apocalyptic noises of police sirens and buildings crashing to the ground. Then, above the high rise blocks on the skyline we saw It – at least three hundred feet high – rampaging along the high street like King Kong.

'My God!' I choked. *'It can't be **that** big! He must be terribly angry for it to be **that** erect!'*

'It's heading for the Birtwhistle Hotel. The conference is on the top floor. Keep your eyes on the road Victoria! You nearly crashed into that man.'

People were streaming over the main road in terror, and cars were reversing in the fast lane. I zigzagged between these, trying not to knock over a large group of women who were staring up at Daddy's member with fascination and

59

anxiety.

'We'll have to leave the car,' I said as crowds of screaming shoppers, fleeing from the monster, made further headway impossible.

As I stepped out of the car, I heard a gigantic crashing noise. The penis was tearing the roof off the hotel and roaring.

'Daddy! No!' Stephanie screamed, waving a bottle over her head.

As we neared the hotel, army and police vehicles screeched to a halt. Troops with rocket launchers ran for cover as the penis ravaged the upper stories of the hotel. We dodged into a doorway as a hail of debris fell around us. The vast column of flesh raked the inside of the hotel with deafening roars, then straightened: a tiny person was wriggling in its mouth:

'Oh no! That's Gretzel!' I shrieked.

But the penis' triumph was short lived. It gave a shrill cry and shuddered along its length. We saw Gretzel falling through the air like a doll. It had dropped her.

'Heeeeeeeeeeeeellllllllllllllllllllllllllpppppppppppppppp!' She yelled, and landed in the hotel awning, ten feet from where we stood. After a long belching rip, Gretzel was dumped onto the pavement, still holding a can of aerosol.

'I sprayed under the foreskin with acid!' she gasped as I helped her to her feet. *'I always carry a can to spray in the eyes of rapists or muggers.'*

I looked round. The penis was slumping onto the street, writhing in agony, and shrinking fast.

'Ouch,' I breathed.

But as soldiers began running out of cover, a taxi careered out of a side street and stopped in a cloud of blue exhaust fumes. A rear door swung open and Father's penis wriggled in. The car screeched away down another side street, bullets

60

zinging in pursuit.

'Stephanie!' I gasped, recognising the driver.

Dazed, I went with Gretzel to the police station.

'The reason men are such pricks,' she announced, to the discomfort of the policeman who was dressing her wounds, *'is that they **have** pricks. They just don't know how to keep them under control.'*

Barely wincing as the severe bites on her arms and legs were bound, Gretzel recounted her story to a rather ugly sergeant who took notes.

'There we were, denouncing penis envy, when all of a sudden we heard this terrible commotion, police sirens, loud crashes, people screaming. Several of us looked out of the window and saw this giant prick coming towards us. All I can remember is saying 'Wow,' before the ceiling was ripped off and I was grabbed by King Dong.'

After Gretzel had finished, I told the story of my Mother and her bottled genitalia. The sergeant wasn't impressed:

'You should have informed us immediately when the Penis attacked its first victim,' he grunted.

'You'd have laughed at me.'

'Stranger things have happened Miss.'

I was about to say, *such as?* when a constable rushed in to inform us that the stolen taxi had been found and that my sister and her fugitive companion were holed up in a deserted farmhouse twenty miles away.

'It's threatening to kill your sister unless it gets a helicopter and half a million in used notes.'

By the time we arrived at the farmhouse, dozens of armed men were deployed in the area, crouching behind decrepit tractors or crumbling stone walls.

'*You don't have to use violence,*' I told a police superintendent, '*I have this bottle of formaldehyde.*'

'*Let them blow the shit out of it,*' Gretzel advised quietly, chewing on a cigar.

'*You're not thinking of Stephanie.*' I said coldly.

'*It will have* **you** *then* **as well**. *It's not worth the risk.*' The superintendent said.

'*I think I can handle my own father's penis,*' I replied haughtily.

Minutes later, I was picking my way determinedly through a dock-festooned farmyard towards the house. The penis watched my approach through a broken window:

'*The door's open,*' It said in a suave voice when I knocked.

Gingerly, I went inside.

Stephanie was in a corner, behind an overturned chair. Her dress was ripped and her face was bruised – as if she were the heroine in a Victorian melodrama.

'*You shouldn't have come in,*' she said, shaking.

The penis – naked and six-foot high was smirking as it slid between myself and the door.

'*The fair Victoria,*' It sneered. '*How is Mummy's girl?*'

'*What have you done to Stephanie?*' I asked, trying to keep calm. '*She rescued you. Your own daughter.*'

'*I told It to give itself up and It went berserk.*'

Again the penis smiled.

'*No more solitary confinement for me. I hope you're not going to suggest the same, dear Victoria? But of course you are. You've come to talk me back into my bottle haven't you?*'

'*No.*'

The penis became suddenly angry:

'*Don't lie to me. I know they're out there. The police, with*' *guns. Surrounding the place. Well you're wasting your breath. You can go back to them and say I don't fear hanging.'*

'Go Victoria.' my sister whimpered, *'while you can.'*

'You've both got it all wrong,' I said. *'There are lots of people out there. Press and photographers, waiting for you Father. Your present incarnation has convinced them that your theories are true.'*

The penis twitched defensively.

'No.'

'You're famous at last. Your advances in the field of psychology have been accepted. The police are trying to protect you from those who want you arrested because of what you did this morning. But you're bigger than Freud. They're laughing at Freud now.'

'You're lying,' said the fleshly monstrosity, but I could see it was becoming flaccid.

I summoned up all my courage and walked over to it.

'What's more, Father, even I accept it.'

Trying not to show my disgust, I put up my hand to stroke the bloated flesh, to comfort it.

'When I saw your magnificence today, your overweening power, dominating an entire town, I was envious.'

'Envious.' It breathed the word in painful triumph: *'It's not true. It can't be.'*

'Even Gretzel said: Wow.'

'Gretzel. That filthy bitch.'

'Is envious too. She admits it. Your theories – they're all vindicated. People want to celebrate your achievements. They're all out there now. You don't ever have to go back into that bottle. That dark cupboard.'

'No.'

The penis grew smaller and smaller. When it was only a foot

long. I sat beside it on the floor.

'They're talking of giving you the Nobel Prize.'

It managed a feeble smile:

'Why not? All the others that got it are pricks.'

Then from its eye – or mouth or whatever it was – the thing began to weep. It shuddered and wept like a little child. And as it lay there, on dirty cracked lino, pathetic and small, I manoeuvred the bottle out of my pocket. In seconds, I picked up the wriggling worm, and poked it down the neck of the bottle. Preservative spurted out as I squeezed the cork home.

Leaving the bottle in the middle of the room, I went and put my coat round Gretzel.

We sat and hugged each other, orphans – together for what seemed like the first time in our lives. We were still like that when the police came in to arrest the bottle and take it away forever.

The Schoolhouse

Old Con limped down the lane after his cows. The sun had burned low and all that was left of the day was flies. Where the herd curved habitually off the road into the farm gate, a Range Rover was waiting to get by. Con whacked his stick on the cows' behinds to hurry them through to the milking shed. In the back of the car, two small children bounced up and down excitedly.

'Cows! Cows!' they shouted:

A boy stuck his head sideways through the gap of a part-opened window:

'Moooo!'

'Tom! Don't do that,' scolded the boy's mother in a BBC accent.

A few days earlier the same family had driven up the road to see the old schoolhouse. Though why foreigners were so keen to buy damp buildings was a mystery to Con. You could raise a new dry one for half the price.

Con's younger brother Declan was hooking up the cows as they came passively into their stalls.

'I see'd 'em agin,' Con said, *'The English fellah an' his wife an' kids. Off up to the old school to have another look.'*

'Did ya?'

'I did.'

Declan seemed disinterested, but asked:

'And were ya talking to 'em?'

'No. They're up there now. Looking round the place. They just stopped for the cows to go by.'

With a stub of straw, Con picked at his two remaining teeth and laughed inwardly as his brother hurried to the milking machine. He knew Declan wanted to go and watch the visitors from behind the school. But the family would be gone by the time the cows were finished. Still, to be sure of it, he'd let Declan scuttle about like a rat without a hole, then give him the woodpile to sort out.

Leaning on his stick, grimacing at pains in his hip, Con left the milking shed. Moments later, Declan peered round the door to be certain his brother had gone and croaked in a tearful high-pitched voice:

'He's seen 'em and I've not.'

By the time Declan finished the jobs his brother had set him, the sky was black and the English family were long gone. He crept over to the school anyhow. Though it bordered his brother's land, Declan seldom went near the place. He had never learned to read or write, and long ago, the schoolteacher Mrs Monahan had tried to beat him through the gates of literacy like an animal into a mart pen. The place hadn't been used as a schoolhouse for thirty years. But it still haunted Declan in a way that others might feel walking round Belsen.

Ten years back, the place had been bought by an artist. A Dutchman who painted all the woodwork yellow and purple. He married an English girl whose face grew longer, the longer she lived there. She said it was the endless rain and low cloud that depressed her, but Declan knew it was the school itself. Many nights Declan had sneaked up to the house hoping to hear or see the couple making love. Instead he heard her wild voice sobbing and the Dutchman shouting at her to stop, slapping her face – like a headmistress slapping a child that couldn't decipher black squiggles on a page. The woman went back to England. Not long after, the Dutchman packed his brushes and left for good. The school fell into disrepair. Kids from the village broke slates by sliding down the roof. The windows were knocked in. Tinkers smashed the door off. But Declan never once went inside. Now an auctioneer's sign hung over the gates. The Dutchman was selling up.

Declan crept up to the school and stood outside, bats veering above him in the hot night. He'd touched his brow to the head teacher Mrs Monahan till the day she died. That day, Con brought the news from the pub. She'd been going down faster than a shot crow, they'd said. But she went peacefully, in her sleep, without so much as a thud. After breaking the news to his brother, Con belched Guinness fumes through the kitchen, and shook his head as if the whole thing were sad. Declan crept barefoot into the cowshed. Stroking a calf, he'd laughed and cried simultaneously.

Late afternoon the next day, the English couple were at the schoolhouse again. The man, in white shorts and sandals, was checking windows for rot. His wife was explaining to the children:

'This must have been the playground.'

The big yard, as if ashamed of its previous existence, was now obscured by willows, nettles, and tall grass. The couple went inside, discussing the dampness of the bathroom. The boy and girl were left playing in the sun. Declan watched, squinting through gaps in a gorse bush. The playground had once milled with all the children of the village. Fifty of them. Screaming. Shrieking. Yells. Often his. They had given him the burns on his first day. Micheal Donovan and the older ones. They'd grabbed his wrists and rubbed his skin tightly in their hands till he cried. And he'd gone running home early. To his father's belt. The next day was the same. Only this time he ran down and hid by the river, till Con had come to find him, shouting that he wasn't in trouble and he wouldn't get hit. But he got the belt just the same. Con had been lying. In the end Declan gave up running off and sneaked around the playground trying not to be seen, so the other children wouldn't tie him up with string and pull him along, or spit in his hair or make him say he loved a girl.

Declan watched the little English boy and his sister throw grass in the air to watch it come down. They were happy as calves before being parted from their mammies, with the innocence of those who do not know what the world is like. Who know nothing of forcible separation, the mart, the slaughterhouse. Or of brothers that kicked the udders of cows that wouldn't drop their milk, when all that was needed was a soft word and a stroke.

Later, as the English family's off-roader went back along the lane, the driver saw Declan standing by a gate. He brought the car to a halt and spoke through the window.

'Hello. I wonder if you could direct us to the nearest shop.'

Declan smiled shyly.

'Y'could try the creamery over at the cross.'

The man in the car couldn't quite grasp the dialect.

'We'd like to get some cold drinks.'

'Oh yes. It's hot. It's hot.'

From the back seat, two children stared with horrified expressions at Declan's toothless mouth and frizzy grey hair that was yellowing like nicotined fingers.

'You'd be wanting to buy the place?'

The Englishman shrugged:

'Well, we're still making up our minds.'

68

He looked back to his wife. From behind dark glasses she smiled reluctantly.

'My name's Peter by the way. Peter Hewitt. And this is my wife Julie. And my two children, Chloe and Tom.'

Declan just nodded, smiled and shook the Englishman's hand as it came out of the window. Peter Hewitt talked on to cover his confusion at the etiquette of this introduction.

'We're just over from England. We've rented a place down by the sea. But we want to buy our own. We thought we could convert the old school.'

'Oh. Yes.'

'There isn't a shop in the village is there?'

'No. You'd want the creamery.'

'And is that far?'

'It's on the cross.'

'Right. Well, er...nice to have met you.'

Declan smiled and gave half a wave as the car scrunched off.

'Where've ya been?' Con demanded when his brother returned.

'I mended a fence that was down.'

'In the schoolhouse?' sneered Con.

'No.'

'Ya spoke to em did ya?'

Declan sat guiltily in his chair by the fireplace.

'I saw ya waitin' for 'em on the road.'

There was a long silence. Declan stared at a large discoloured stain on the wallpaper. Con spread a paper on the table and read, picking his nose. After a while, he spoke again:

'They're buying it off the Dutch fellah are they then?'

'I don't know. They just asked fer the creamery.'

Con broke open a bottle of Guinness. The top rattled on the

wooden table. He poured the stout gently into a glass, nurturing coarse bubbles to a head. After a long sup he wiped froth from his top lip and belched with relish.

'Well I don't want ya talking to 'em agin. They'd not be interested in the likes o'you.'

Con drank deep, his throat moving like a lizard's. Declan kept on looking at the brown wallpaper stain, but shifted uneasily in his seat. Con drained the glass and banged it on the table, then stood as if to leave. Quickly, in his croaky high voice Declan muttered:

'It does no harm. Just talking.'

In a sudden fury, Con shouted:

'You'll do as I tell ya! Alright?'

He hurled the empty bottle into the fireplace. It smashed and a curved fragment landed rocking at Declan's feet.

'It's my farm. If ya don't like it, go sleep in a ditch.'

He stood over Declan, who cowered, like an insect crossed by a shadow. Then before Con could hit him, he sprang from the chair, his back bent almost into a question mark and scuttled from the house. He didn't dare weep in front of Con. That only made him hit harder.

Heavy blasts of rain were breaking the spell of good weather. Shouting in his cracked voice, Declan was beaten down the road by the squall:

'I niver said a word to 'em. Niver one word. You've no right to bate me.'

He ran blindly. Rain seeped icily down his collar. He saw the old school and ran to shelter inside. For a while he shivered in the hall, but eventually grew so cold that he ventured into one of the old classrooms to make a fire. There he caught his breath, for it still *smelt the same.* That mouldy stink that had offended his nostrils for so, so many years. By the light of a match, he peered at the raised platform where the teacher had sat. The windows were six foot up the walls so the children couldn't look out. Then he walked, into the adjoining classroom, broken glass crunching underfoot. It was just as he remembered it. But all so tiny. He struck match after match just to marvel – like Gulliver in Lilliput – at the smallness of everything. He couldn't believe he had ever felt awe for the place. Now, as he thought of Mrs Monahan, it occurred to him that she had been a little old woman. He could have broken her in his hands like a twig.

'Read it!' Slap. *'Read it!'* Slap. *'Read it boy!'* Slap. Slap. Slap. Many times she had stung his tear-streaked face with her palm, until he became hysterical, then she'd thrown him out of the schoolhouse doors.

'Ya old bitch.'

She had taught Con to read. How different everything would be had she not. Declan felt the dead schoolteacher's presence in the darkness, still regarding him with disdain. His squeaky voice shouted:

*'Ya bitch, ya should've taught **me**!'*

He lit a match and held it up to the blackness, as if to singe the dead schoolteacher's face. Then dropped it. For lights flashed against the windows. There was the sound of a car approaching.

Like a startled animal, Declan scrambled mewling into the small room at the back of the building. It had once been Mrs Monahan's office. He cowered in the pitch black, biting his knuckles. A door slammed. For a few minutes he could hear nothing but his own blood pumping in his ears. He tried to press himself into the walls. A muffled woman's voice was saying:

*'I think Chloe's right. It **is** creepy. Even more so at night.*

Shine the torch Peter...'

'Yes but not when all our things are here it won't be.'

The man's voice sounded exasperated.

They went back into the first classroom. Declan breathed easier. But then light slow steps pattered close to him. The door creaked open. A light flashed in. Declan flinched as a child screamed. The scream was the most terrible thing he'd ever heard. Worse than when his father had hung the pig upside down to slash its throat. A torch dropped onto the floor and the door slammed.

'Mummy!' shrieked a girl's voice. 'Mummy! Help me! There's a man! There's a horrible man!'

Two adults shouted.

'Chloe! Chloe!'

'There's a horrible man in the room! Get me out!'

Her shrill cries sent Declan shaking into a corner. He could hear the girl being taken outside and longed for the car engine to drown out her hysterical sobbing. Instead there came the sound of cautious footsteps returning.

'Hello? Is there anybody around? Hello?'

Peter Hewitt shone his torch into the room. Declan whimpered fearfully, thinking the man was going to beat him,

'Are you okay?'

The torch dazzled brighter as Hewitt approached.

'We didn't know you were in here. What happened? Do you need help? We wanted to see what the place felt like at night. Were you sheltering from the rain?'

Through tears the old man stammered:

'I went to school here.'

Baffled, Hewitt tried to help Declan, but his legs wouldn't straighten.

'Look, are you hurt?'

A fresh outburst of screaming came from outside.

'I'm sorry. I must go.'

Declan suddenly grabbed Hewitt's wrist.

'Don't tell my brother I was talking to ya.'

'What?'

'Don't tell Con. He'll bate me.'

'Please. Let go.'

The Englishman twisted free, then extremely perturbed, went quickly from the room.

Footsteps retreated, squeaking on smashed glass. A car engine roared and faded into the night. When the sound of it was gone, Declan scrabbled for wood and paper. He ripped and heaved at rotten floorboards, piling them up. Then he lit a match and nurtured flames – all the time muttering:

'Ya hated children. Ya bate 'em. Ya bate me. Day after day. Like we was cattle. It was worse'n a cowshed. I wouldn't bring a child in here. There's niver a happy child come out of here. Niver. Well ya'll niver do it agin. Not now I'm going to burn ya place ter Hell.'

He watched the blaze grow, then made off through the classrooms to the front door. As he stepped outside, a hand grabbed him by the scruff. Declan yelped. Con spat:

'What did I say about speaking to them people?'

'I didn't niver say a thing. I was sheltering from the rain and they came in.'

Con shook his brother violently.

'Why was the child crying?'

'I don't know.'

'Come on!'

'She just came in, an she seed me there, an I niver did say a thing!'

Con whipped his brother with a stick, driving him down the

73

steps with ferocious blows:

'Ya liar! Why did she scream?'

Doubled over and wailing, Declan raised an arm to protect himself. But as Con lifted the stick again he saw orange shadows at the school windows. Smoke bulged out of a broken pane.

'What have ya done?'

In that moment Declan dodged off through the school gates. Con went a few steps after him, then turned back to stop the fire.

'Ya feckin eejit, what've ya done?'

In his long steps, like a wet cranefly, Declan stumbled down to the river. There was a hole in the roots of a willow where he'd hidden as a child. From this damp earthy lie, he watched the horizon glow over the schoolhouse and repeated:

'I only did it to for to save them two kids from that dead bitch.'

He knew that he would soon hear Con's voice ringing out of the darkness telling him to come on home and that he wasn't in trouble. But this time, he would know it was lies. The place was burning to a shell, and no matter what Con said, he would stay hidden and sleep in the ditch.

The Man who Thought he was in
a Short Story

Dermott woke and knew instantly that he was in a short story. His first feeling was despair. At least in a novel you got a decent life span. He sat up in bed and looked around. He was in a bedsit. A pile of greasy washing-up looked as if it had crash-landed in the sink. There was something about the room which suggested 'victim'. Murder even. The thought of being chopped up in a grisly mystery-type story was enough to get Dermott springing out of bed. It was freezing! He pulled on jeans with a hole in the knee. He could see his own breath. But for how long? He ransacked drawers for something warm. All his jumpers seemed shoddy and unravelling. He couldn't believe he was such a pathetic character.

He knew it was imperative to get out of the room and find a place where murder would be less easily carried out. And he needed to find a bookshop so that he could browse the short story section. Maybe he could find his own story on the shelves to see what happened.

Dermott listened at the door. He opened it stealthily. The landing smelt of old carpets, stale cigarettes and students generally. He crept down two flights of stairs, opened the front door and screamed: A man was holding a key up to the lock. Like it was a gun! Dermott fled past him in terror.

'Dermott! Are you okay!' the man shouted in bewilderment.

But Dermott was already halfway down the street, running. After a while he slowed to a fast walk, flinching as other pedestrians went by. Somehow, knew where he was. He was heading for the main street in Cork City. Cars nosing down thin streets beside him were becoming so numerous that it was now futile to hide in doorways as they went by. Not one of them had machine-gunned him yet anyway.

Once on Patrick Street Dermott felt a little safer and he was now struck by the thought that things could definitely be worse. He *could* be one of the faceless crowds of shoppers drifting past. None of them even seemed to know they were in a work of fiction. Poor sods. To be walk-on parts in a short story. What a terribly empty and meaningless fate!

Then Dermott saw Waterstones. A bookshop! An old woman held the door open for him, but he used another – he wasn't going to get knifed as easily as all that. The shop was full of comatose people staring at shelves. No one looked round as he came in, though as a central character, Dermott felt pretty conspicuous. Fiction. Short fiction. That's what he needed.

Dermott frantically scanned the shelves. What would *his* collection be called? *Nice Things That Happened To Dermott...* Probably not. He wondered what sort of things actually happened in modern short stories and picked up an anthology. After two pages he felt sleepy. Nothing had happened. Suddenly he turned – just to catch any would-be assassins in mid-stab. An assistant nearby looked at him quizzically.

'It's okay,' shrugged Dermott trying to look casual. *'I'm just in a short story......Y'know......'*

The assistant went off, looking back twice at Dermott before reaching the counter. Time was running out. The story could be almost halfway through and Dermott still wasn't sure what genre he was in...... *Then he found it!* A blank cover. A slim volume. Almost forgotten amongst the glossy brilliance of the other titles. The words of the first story ran...

'Dermott woke and knew instantly that he was in a short story....'

It was gripping stuff. To Dermott anyway. He'd read two paragraphs when he decided to skip to the end. Then he noticed a young woman was standing rather close to him. He moved over to let her get a better look at the shelves. She moved next to him again and said:

'Would you mind if I had a look? It's about me too.'

Dermott gorped. She *knew!* No one else had the least idea they were fictional but this woman...He handed her the book.

'Shall we buy it?' she asked.

Dermott fumbled in his pockets for money. *'I've got one pound fifty...'* he offered, lamely.

'It won't be more than that.' she said, taking the money, adding somewhat brutally: *'It's only cheap stuff.'*

She walked to the counter. Dermott hurried after her: she was incredibly cool and attractive.

'My name's Dermott,' said Dermott as the till went *ching.*

'I **know** *that!'* she said. *'I'm Mairead'.*

She walked out of the shop and into crowds of people.

'Where are we going?' asked Dermott, assuming that she wouldn't mind him tagging along as they had been thrown together in such an extraordinary way.

'To read the end, of course.'

'But **where?***'* said Dermott, still paranoid.

She stopped and looked at him.

'You can come to my place for a coffee if you like? We can read it there.' Dermott felt her eyes go right into his own, brushing away any possible barriers between them. But they'd only just met! She walked on, and he followed dry mouthed,

plucking up the courage to ask another question.

'I don't suppose you er...know......you know...what...er... genre we're in?'

She sighed as if at his uselessness:

'Romantic comedy.'

Dermott felt his heart gallop. He forgot he was in a short story and had a good look at himself in a shop window as he passed. His reflection was scruffy, but good-looking in a scrawny sort of way. And *she*...well she was......

'Er do we...do we....um......?'

She slotted a key into a door.

'Oh yes, several cups.'

Dermott followed her into a dark hallway. Her flat was on the ground floor. She went in and put the kettle on, throwing the book carelessly onto her bed. Dermott tried to think of something to say.

'What do you do?'

'Oh I just work at a chemists. Behind the counter.' She made a face and set a cup of coffee in front of him. *'Hurry up. I'm going to drink mine in bed.'*

She slipped between the covers and flipped through the pages of the slender white volume. Dermott scalded his tongue in haste to join her.

'Right,' he said. *'Don't miss anything...er...romantic.'*

'I won't. There's only a couple of lines left anyway.'

'What?' He jumped up and made for the bed before it was too late. But his legs buckled.

'Mairead laughed' laughed Mairead, reading aloud. *'She'd poisoned his coffee......'*

She looked down at the choking Dermott.

'I lied about the genre.'

Ophelia

22nd April. When I first revealed to other people that I was Shakespeare reincarnated, they laughed. They'd always come up with some ridiculous question:

'How come you don't write fantastic plays then?'

But there's always people going round claiming they're Jesus, and can they do miracles? I got slagged off in my first life as a young upstart, then later generations saw that I was dead poetic. It means *nothing* that my masterpieces of this century are given terrible reviews. In a couple of hundred years time, my more recent history plays like *Hitler The First* will be seen as classics. The same goes for my *Laming Of The Gnu*.

29th April. My psychiatrist Henry, keeps asking me how I know I'm a great playwright, when all the reviews of my work point to the contrary. He even quotes the newspapers to me:

'The Flat Calm is one of the worst plays I've ever witnessed in my life. The writer should be shot with a blunderbuss full of seagull ordure.'

And:

'The Suicidal Wives Of Windsor is almost as bad as *Brothello.* Theatre so bad that you wonder the audience didn't slit their wrists with boredom.'

Yet – as I tell Henry frequently – I can remember every

detail of my past life. Even doing it with Anne Hathaway in that little Stratford cottage. The colour of her dress that I took off was brown, and she had a wart on her knee.

6th May. I only started writing this diary because Henry told me I should get all my 'delusions' (as he calls them) down on paper. It's very helpful, because once my quill has got them down in black and white, I can see much more clearly that I'm entirely right. I told Henry today about the new play I am writing – *Ophelia*. I began, as always, by lying down on his leather couch and reciting some of my former work – *Shall I compare thee to a summer's day?* This always seems to irritate Henry. He was quite nice when we first started talking, but he's been increasingly tetchy lately. He wants to go back to my dead father's obsession with Shakespearean verse, which is quite dull for me. Okay, my second dad was obsessed with work I'd done before he was born. But that seems perfectly natural. I was much more interested in explaining to Henry why I'd made such a hash of getting Ophelia's story onto paper the first time. But as I started to expand on my latest theories on tragedy, Henry went bonkers. He started hitting me with this big thick book about mental illness, and said I was the craziest mad person he'd ever met. I was a little hurt at first but realised that it must be all part of the treatment here in the hospital.

7th May. As I wasn't allowed to explain my theories to Henry face to face, I might as well write them here. If I leave my diary in his office, he might pick it up, read it and *understand*. I realised when I went back over *Hamlet* (my first revision for 400 years), that I'd made a bodge of the whole thing. It's supposed to be a tragedy, but I think I really ballsed up the cathartic effect. Look at it this way: say, back in Elizabethan times, I'd been walking through some back streets in London after half-completing a masterpiece. Then suddenly, a bloody great horse and cart had galloped speeding out of nowhere and flattened me in the mud, severing my head and splattering my guts. That would have been a bit tragic. But if I'd just been staggering back from the Mermaid with a skinful inside me and wandered under a passing horse and cart of my own drunken stupidity – well that would serve me right! The audience only gets a cathartic response when an *innocent* suffers. When a posh privileged prince murders an old codger, fails to avenge his murdered dad, and sends his girlfriend crackers (then into the nearest river for a flowery drowning) well he forfeits any right to *my* sympathy! I can't think *what* I was playing at.

8th May. Henry was right – writing it all down helps get things in their true perspective. I've been awake all night, thinking how badly I treated Ophelia in the first draft of that play. I'm definitely changing the title from *Hamlet*. The publishers will probably kick up a bit of a fuss – all those millions of books having to be recalled. But it's so obvious to me now that *she* is the tragic heroine. Hamlet just gatecrashed the script. Bloody opportunist prima donna.

13th May. I saw Henry again today. He apologised for hitting me with a book. I told him that all famous writers have to get used to brickbats. His eye started twitching and he reached for the book again, his hands trembling. Then started talking about my early life. Why does he keep harping on about my mum and dad? I've told him dozens of times about them being merchants from Stratford and them taking me to see travelling players at the fair. But he wanted to talk about my *other* parents, the 'professors' of literature who brought me up the second time. He asked me if I thought it was normal for a parent to insist on a child reciting sonnets before taking a seat at the breakfast table. I said:

'If your child is a reincarnated Shakespeare, then of course.'

'But your name......' His eye-tic was going like billy-o'. *'...Don't you think William Shakespeare is an odd name for a baby?'*

'Not if he is William Shakespeare,' I said, reasonably enough.

He made a strangled noise in his throat:

'But how would they know?'

I shrugged:

'Maybe they were my first parents reincarnated as well?'

He punched the wall. Then told me to go. I didn't get to say anything about *Ophelia*. I'm beginning to suspect that he is a reincarnated Christopher Marlowe.

14th May. Of course if he *is* a reincarnated Christopher Marlowe, then everything *makes sense.* It must bug him like anything to know that I'm the famous one from the seventeenth century and not him. No wonder he just wants to talk about my parents from the 1960s. They never wrote *any* plays, so I suppose they wouldn't be so galling to discuss. Now I understand Henry's psychology, I think I might be able to help him.

15th May. I told Henry that I often hear voices in my head, and he asked me to transcribe what they say as exactly as possible. Here's one I often get, Polonius praying to me because I am his creator:

Dear William, thank you – oh thank you! I was really upset when you didn't let me do the stabbing in Julius Caesar*, you knew that. But I see you were only saving me up to kill me instead as a tragic hero in* Polonius*. Brilliant title, don't you see? I thought of all kinds of exciting ways that I could die: a plague of wasps trained by Claudius to swarm up my nostrils and sting the inside of my brain. Or being bitten by a duck with a poisoned bill! Now, the play could be about how my household collapses because of my daughter (who never obeys me and who quickly disappears). Her role could be quite small. And then there could be a boorish son who never does anything dramatic, and a walk-on part for Hamlet. Then he could walk off. Whatever you do make sure you rewrite the bit about me being stabbed behind a curtain by mistake, it's so humiliating.*

16th May. I'm writing *Ophelia* so quickly, my quill can hardly keep up with my mind. I've thrown out most of the first stupid plot that I wrote. It's still gory, but now I've got Hamlet trying to murder Ophelia so that he can have the main role in the play. All the other blokes want to kill her too. Polonius woke me up in the middle of the night urging me to scribble her out of the script because she sleeps around. Laertes (his son in the first version, but a cleaner in my latest draft) butted in:

*'Tis an offence to my masculinity to have a woman overshadowing **me**, the star. And I'm not mopping Elsinore's bathrooms.'*

I must admit, I was overcome at my own genius, when I realised that the play is symbolic of the struggle for power that women face in the 21st century. The tragedy is that she is oppressed by the sexism of the men in the play.

20th May. Saw Henry today. We got along like a pyromaniac's house. Now I know he's Christopher Marlowe, I tried to steer clear of talking about my work. I let him talk about my parents to his heart's content. This seemed to relax him a lot. He almost smiled when I didn't recite a sonnet when lying on the couch. Then I answered all his questions about my second parents. He was very pleased about this. Especially when I told him that my mum and dad wallpapered my room with pages torn from the complete works of my former self. He also seemed delighted when I remembered getting a codpiece and a ruff for my seventh birthday. He asked if I'd cried. I told him it had been very upsetting, as they didn't fit. When I left at the end of my hour, he didn't swear at me, which shows that my new theory about him is correct. He said I was making progress, and looked a little surprised when I replied:

'So are you.'

23rd May. I've written a large sex scene in which Ophelia sleeps with both Rozencrantz and Guildenstern. Hamlet is furious:

'William. You've got to stop! I won't tolerate this!' he said, this morning. *'No way is that strumpet Ophelia taking over my play. The rest of the characters are up in arms. The ghost says he won't haunt in this new play unless Ophelia is punished for her unseemly want of chastity.'*

When I told him that she was going to have it off with the gravediggers too, he was apoplectic:

'Over my dead body!'

I said it would have to be, as them doing it with Ophelia at her own funeral would be a lapse in taste.

'Villain!' he yelled. *'I'm going to tell all the others in the play. You'll have a mass revolt on your hands. We'll be avenged!*

Forsooth!'

I immediately wrote in a scene in which Hamlet drowns himself after catching Claudius and Ophelia in an embrace and finding his role in the play usurped by the woman he once loved. Her making love with the gravediggers on Hamlet's coffin will have to be the penultimate scene.

27th May. Answered all of Henry's questions about my childhood this afternoon. What a morbid guy! He wanted all the gruesome details of how my father submerged my mother in the bath after finding she'd slept with his best friend and misquoted *Much Ado About Nothing*. When it was time for me to go, he asked why I hadn't mentioned my play for two whole weeks, and if I was still writing. I didn't want him to know I knew his real identity, though I did call him 'Chris baby' a couple of times by accident. I told him that I'd nearly finished Ophelia, despite having problems with some of the characters.

'But why haven't you wanted to talk about it?'

He was very persistent, (envious maybe that I'd completed another masterpiece so quickly). So, I had to tell him:

'Because I know you're Christopher Marlowe and my genius makes you jealous.'

For some reason, he groaned and clawed his face. Then he yelled:

'Get out you bloody imbecile!!!!!'

'Okay Chris,' I said. *'Don't blow your top.'*

28th May. Crisis! Revolt! As I wrote the final scene of *Ophelia* the male characters tried to stop me. At first it was just Hamlet and Claudius, wheedling:

'Come on Bill, we're old mates. After four hundred years close friendship, we should be able to sort this out without a

load of fuss. Forsooth.'

I kept on writing, blotting ink all over the place in my haste. When they found I was ignoring them, both characters started making threats:

'Bill...' said Hamlet, *'put the quill down, nice and slow. Don't make us get nasty.'*

'Put the quill down, or the girl gets it.' said Claudius.

Still I scribbled like a demon.

'We'll call in the rest of the boys,' snarled Hamlet. *'It won't be pretty...Claudius...'*

Claudius began shouting for the other characters from the first script: *'Fortinbras! Horatio! Osric! Ghost! Rosencrantz! Guildenstern!*

The entire gang of them started shouting inside my brain:

'We'll send you mad,' said Hamlet. *'Yes! Just like you did to me!'*

'I didn't send you mad!' I replied. *'You only pretended to be mad'*

Hamlet raved:

'I went mad with the pretending!'

Then the cast began shouting at me:

'Loony! Loony!'

I suddenly got worried that all these vicious guys in my head might drive me mad, so I yelled:

'No! You won't stop me! You'll never drive me insane! I'm too level headed! Too grounded in reality!'

'Unbrace his doublet!' Polonius shouted.

'Foul his stockings!' roared Horatio.

'Knock his knees together!' Osric giggled.

I couldn't help it, even as I was writing, I couldn't stop my hands undoing my shirt and pulling off my socks.

'Leave me alone!' I screamed, *'I must finish the play. The*

play's the thing!'

'Look at you,' laughed Hamlet, 'You're already a gibbering wreck. The nurses are coming for you. They've heard you shouting. They'll take you to England. Ha Ha! And we'll kill Ophelia!'

I strove to write another fumbling sentence, but began to speak with Hamlet's voice:

'I have of late, but wherefore I know not, – lost all my mirth!'

I felt nurses pulling at my arms, but held on to my quill and paper.

'It goes so heavily with my disposition.'

They were dragging me along saying:

'It's alright William, it's going to be alright.'

Even as I was dragged into a corridor, I was writing furiously. In the final scene, I knew Ophelia had to kill *them*. All the men, it was the only way she could be free. I struggled out of the nurses' hands and wrote on the floor, giving her a bottle of poison in the stage directions, in between yelling:

'The earth seems to me a sterile promontory, the sky a foul and pestilent congregation of vapours!'

The nurses dragged me along the corridor. Then suddenly, I realised I was in Henry's office. He had a syringe in his hand and was saying:

'Now William, you seem very upset, you're just going to have a little sleep. Put down the quill and the paper.'

'Revenge tragedy, Christopher....' I spat, '...is a pathetically macho art form.'

This was Marlowe getting his own back for being 400 years in my shadow: trying to stop my play being finished because he was envious of my talent. The characters in my head roared:

'We've won!'

87

I could hear Ophelia sobbing somewhere. I handed Marlowe my quill and scroll.

'*Alright,*' I said. '*I'll lie on the couch and you can do your worst. Let go of me.*'

But as Christopher turned to set my quill and scroll on his desk, and the nurses released my arms, I threw off my antic disposition. I grabbed a dagger from Marlowe's desk — something I'd seen him use to open letters — and went to plunge it into his back, but he turned and ducked so that the blade went into his eye. The nurses screamed, and when I turned on them with the knife, they ran out. I locked the door, and looked down at Chris. He groaned and slumped in a pool of his own blood:

'*Some people never learn Marlowe,*' I said. '*No matter how many lives they live.*'

Then I sat at his desk and finished the play. As Ophelia poisoned all the men in Elsinore, they fell silent from my mind.

20th June. Ophelia thanked me all the way to the secure psychiatric prison. She said she's had to wait 400 years for Justice. We talk to each other most days. I can even see her in my mind now. She's very lovely, with a face very like my mother's. She suspects the new psychiatrist I've been seeing is actually a reincarnated Ben Jonson. I wonder if he's having problems getting his modern plays critically acclaimed too? I'll bring it up at our next meeting.

Revolver

Eleanor Rigby placed a black disc on the spindle of her gramophone *again*. It was the latest recording by the Beatles: *Revolver.* She brought the stylus over to the second track and listened. How did they know her name? She had been to the Cavern Club, screamed at their concerts and bought every single – but she had never met any of them. Now here was a record about her. How did they know she was lonely? That she lived in a dream? That she kept her face in a jar by the door? It was like a kind of déjà vu. She didn't dare ask the local priest – Father Mackensie – about supernatural forms of communication, because the record said she died in his church. Anyway, he was a creep. Always trying to get past the front door, or stopping her in the street with invitations to meet God.

It had taken Eleanor all her nerve to go up to the church that day to see the wedding of Ringo. She'd stood beside her mother's grave and watched laughing crowds throw rice and confetti. Later, she sadly bent down to screw up the rice that had been thrown. Then that sort of déjà vu swamped everything. She ran home and fell on the bed screaming. *Picking up the rice was in the song.* Now she was sure to die. The whole crazy thing was sending her mad, paranoid, despairing. Eleanor wanted to smash the record. But couldn't. She kept playing that second track compulsively and handling the revolver with which she planned to kill Father Mackensie. As the music belted out, Eleanor went into one of her dreams:

'Who was the weird chick watching from the cemetery?' **Ringo asked his new wife as the limousine purred down Penny Lane towards the docks. He'd been so high during the ceremony; he'd put the wedding ring through his nose saying:**

'There's no room on me fingers Father.'

Then on the way out of the church he'd seen this woman with no face holding a jam jar. It was the one discordant note in the whole proceedings. But his wife wasn't listening. She was being shaved by a barber. They were going down to the docks. Liverpool looked black and white as those early suits. Only people holding psychedelic flowers, heading down to board the Yellow Submarine splashed a little colour. Ringo kissed his wife and felt the sun giggle as he stepped out of the car. There was shaving foam on his lips.

Back in her room, Eleanor wept. She was going to miss the Yellow Submarine. It was leaving without her. She didn't have the courage to go up there and shoot Mackenzie. Though she knew it was the only way the future could be made different from the song. Instead she took the face from its jar and threw it across the room.

'I hate you! I hate you Eleanor!'

When she picked it up it had a nosebleed. It was an ugly face anyway. She had been saving it for Ringo. Not the most sought after or fashionable of the Fab Four. But he was a sad clown who would understand her and tell those stupid jokes. She had been saving the face for him and now he had gone and got married. The moron. It was hypocrisy, this singing plaintively about lonely people. When one of them could have married her. They knew she was lonely. They'd written the song for God's sake. As Eleanor wept, tears mingled with the nasal blood.

Where do they all come from? Eleanor lay on the bed and saw all the lonely people floating through space, drifting like weird spores down to earth. People who had never had anyone, or anything other than an isolated floating through star-struck darkness. Lonely people. They had never been hugged. Held as if they really mattered to somebody. No mother or father. None that noticed them anyhow. Just space all around them. Nothing that would anchor them to others. Desolate empty drifting down. And they belonged nowhere. She had kidded herself that she had belonged with Ringo. From huge posters of him in her room, he gazed out at her with that lovely gormless smile. But all the time he had been in love with a model. A woman of glamour and no substance, who would never appreciate his brilliant drumming. Eleanor rose to tear down the posters. She hated Ringo. She had always hated him. Her fingernails slashed through the posters as if through his skin. How cruel of them to write that song. Then she was dreaming again. Though it was still in the dock, she could see the Yellow Submarine's destination. Her dream moved ahead of time:

'Are you sure the Maharishi knows where he's driving us George?'

John was looking out of a porthole at a walrus swimming past. Somewhere, a brass band was pounding out that all you need is Love. Eleanor saw her mother, through the porthole, swimming with a revolver and shooting at an octopus. There was a small child wrapped in rags drowning at the bottom of the sea, amongst oysters applauding with their shells. Eleanor knew that she was the child, and that her mother was swimming away because she had no love

91

left. Her mother was swimming away to kill herself. As Eleanor wept she found that George was somehow holding her around the waist and stroking her like a guitar.

'*Lonely people come from mothers who can't love, and fathers who run away....*' she sang to John as he went past. But John didn't seem to hear. He was climbing a ladder. Beautiful people were pouring from the submarine onto a field full of giant strawberries. There was a boat on a river, tangerine trees, marmalade skies...

And then the dream stopped. Eleanor came spinning back to the ugliness of her terraced home. If she could only board the Yellow Submarine before it submerged, she wouldn't be lonely any more. *She had to kill Mackensie.*

Eleanor gripped the army revolver that had blown her suicidal mother's brains against the wall. Then she slipped out of the door. Kids were laughing as they kicked a football in the street. She hurried past them to Mackensie's house, beside the church. Dim lights shone in both front rooms. Round the back of the house, the door was open. Scarcely breathing, Eleanor crept over the kitchen lino and into the hall. A grandfather clock ticked loudly. Was Mackensie still in the church? With trepidation, she turned the handle of the study door. No one there. She tiptoed in and picked up the telephone.

'*Hello? I'd like to order a taxi. Miss Rigby. Father Mackensie's house by the church.*'

She replaced the receiver and looked down at a sheet of paper on Mackenzie's writing desk. It was part of the sermon that no-one would hear:

...The traditional Christian ways of life have been destroyed by a godless modernity, which started with a false idolatry for the Beatles pop group. The values and lifestyle propounded by

such immoral young people have led to society falling apart. The idea of free love has led to the most sacred acts between man and wife being committed by anyone on a whim. Fathers and mothers no longer stay together and heed their responsibilities. And where does this leave the children? Those who will build the society of tomorrow? They are left in loneliness and despair. Without love and guidance from the natural authority of their own parents. What kind of world will grow from such a beginning? Only a sad fragmented unspiritual world...

Eleanor looked up at a creaking floorboard. There was Mackensie standing in freshly darned socks.

'I'm glad to find you here Eleanor.'

She grasped the gun in her coat pocket. But said:

'I was just going Father.'

She tried to walk past him, but he didn't move from the doorway.

'Why did you come here? Was it to speak to me? For comfort in God?'

'I've got to go Father. A taxi's coming to take me away.'

'You read my sermon. Did you agree with it?'

Eleanor flushed.

'Father. Have you heard **Revolver**?'

Mackensie looked at her strangely.

'Why do you ask that?'

'Have you heard the song about us?'

'What song?'

She suddenly barged past him, blindly – colliding with a wall. Mackensie was shouting at her.

'Eleanor! Eleanor! Stop!'

He tried to catch hold of her, but she struggled free and ran to a door which led into the church. Mackensie was stumbling behind her in the gloom. She realised that this was the place where the song said she would die, and became hysterical – screaming and turning amidst an aisle of pews. Mackensie grabbed and shook her.

'What is it child! What is it!'

'You're going to kill me! You're going to kill me!'

He held her by the arms and shouted into her snot-strewn face.

'Eleanor. I won't. I'm your father. Your own father, do you hear me? Do you understand?'

This made her quiet. Eleanor wriggled from his grasp.

'What are you talking about?'

Mackensie wrung his trembling hands.

'Eleanor, do you believe that people make mistakes and can be forgiven? I am your father. I sinned long ago with your mother. We could never get married. I tried to stop her letting out our secret about you. That we had a child together. She forced me to be harsh. I couldn't let it be known. Not in my position. So I forbade her. I was cruel to her. And that's why......why...she took my revolver. My army revolver that I'd had in the war......and...she killed......

He stopped. Eleanor looked at him in horror.

'No.' she said. *'Not you. You are **not** my father.'*

'But Eleanor, we have the same faces – we...'

Mackensie took off his face. Underneath it was blank. Just like hers. He even had a jar. Eleanor screamed and pulled the revolver from her coat. Then backed away from him, down the pews. Tripping.

'No! That's not true!'

She held the gun to her head. Mackensie shouted, but his words were drowned in an echoing explosion.

There was blood on the songbooks. Mackensie couldn't look

and ran from the church. Outside, a newspaper taxi was burning on the road. Ashes blew into the night like the scatterings of his own condemned soul. Mackensie knelt beside the flames and howled. As if to find Hell, he plunged his bare hands into the burning paper wanting the lesser pain to drive guilt out of his mind. His scorched hands were left holding a charred fragment of tomorrow's newspaper obituary, which said: *Eleanor Rigby.*

Confessions of a Deckchair

I always felt that being a deckchair didn't suit me. That somehow, by having to support heavy posteriors for hours on a hot day, I'd been miscast in the great scheme of the Universe. It's not as if people were even grateful. They'd fold me with a clack after a good sit and walk out of my life as if we'd never been intimately involved. I felt used. Then there were the long lonely winters. Left out in the rain. Seeing comrades rot and end up on a skip. No wonder I got bitter.

After ten years, I changed from a youthful blue and white striped chair – easy to set up and reliable – into a slippery nightmare that would flatten on the sand the moment a customer descended. My favourite noise was a disc slipping. The groans of spread-eagled victims were my delight. I suppose I too would have ended up on the scrap heap, if it hadn't have been for an eighteen-stone beer slob called Tony. I *knew* I was superior to this belching heap of lard in swimming trunks, and after six hours of him snoring on me, I could bear Tony no longer. Something in me snapped. I whacked together like a mousetrap and swallowed him in a gulp.

I didn't expect people to be so tasty. That pink flesh, lightly fried in suntan oil, factor-seven, sent my stripes psychedelic. I told myself that humans were junk food and bad for the digestion. But a week later, a retired postman ended his holiday abruptly in mid-snooze. After that I found I just couldn't resist a nibble when somebody slumped down on me.

Mostly I ate nice old ladies and snoring grandads. There's not much to chew on a child, and lifeguards would struggle too pugnaciously on the way down. But my steady consumption of people led to weird side effects. Deckchairs as a rule are not big eaters. They hunt at night in flocks, snapping at moths, gnats, and the occasional wild duck. By eating as much as twenty stone of human flesh a day, I started to grow. Nobody noticed at first, but when I reached twenty-five feet tall, and customers needed a ladder to get in to me, I could see my owner getting suspicious. If I hadn't eaten him you see, he would have grassed. The disappearance of 127 sunbathers from a single beach over the summer hadn't gone *entirely* unnoticed. I fought to cut humans out of my diet. I tried to talk to other chairs, to get help, but to no avail. I thought about clattering down to the end of the pier and throwing myself off. But I knew I'd just float. The bigger I grew, the more people stared. It was only a matter of time before I was caught.

So one midnight, I took off, migrating like so many deckchairs before me, to Brighton. I hoped to meet other carnivorous chairs and form a stack. I got as far as Totnes before dawn, and hid in a tree-lined garden. It was a warm day, and after a while, a fleshless old man came out to read his morning paper. He was carrying the cutest little rocking chair I'd ever seen. She was so ornate and delicate that I felt hot all over and started to flap. Peeking through the foliage, I could hear her sighing as she bore the grandad's uncomfortable bony bottom. Once he was gone, I emerged:

'Hi. I'm Declan.'

She fell over in shock. I helped her up. The moment she was in my embrace I kissed her.

'Oh you're such a tall, handsome deckchair. Just like I

always dreamed of.'

Much has been written about love, but humans have it pretty bleak in comparison to us chairs. As Chi-chi's arms went around me, rose petals burst spontaneously from a nearby bush and twirled down upon us. Though it was near midday, the sun set and a flock of nightingales serenaded us with Chopin's Etude no. 3. We fused into one chair, climaxing in a shower of multi-coloured sparks.

Chairs gestate much quicker than humans, and we'd hardly finished when Chi-chi gave birth to a little stack of kids. They looked just like their mother, but with my stripes. I was so proud I clacked around the trees shouting: *'Yippee! I'm a dad!'*

Which was a mistake because it brought the old johnny out to investigate. I was peckish from romping with Chi-chi, so I gobbled him up and offered her a torn-off leg. To my amazement, she screamed, and ran off with the kids:

'What's wrong mom?' they asked, galloping after her.

I followed her into the house, crashing through the french windows because of my height.

'Chi-chi! Listen! I love you. Why are you getting so hysterical about a measly little human? Don't you know how evil they are? They torture animals to test their make-up. They eat nice little baa lambs. Harpoon cuddly whales. How many beautiful beaches have been polluted by their sewage?'

She quietened down just as neighbours came to investigate the sounds of bursting glass. I ate all four humans in a snarling passion. Chi-chi even helped me polish off some left over hands. Then I heard sirens: I was too full to cram down a dessert of policemen. There was no time to hide, I just stood still in the garden, and Chi-chi sat with the kids in the house. Before long two policemen came nosying by.

'No sign of anyone Sarge.'

98

'Neighbours are gone too. The ones who phoned us. But there's four cups of coffee steaming in the kitchen.'

The sergeant looked puzzled. 'Anything stolen or broken?'

'No Sarge. Only the french windows busted in and this bloody great deckchair in the garden.'

As Sarge examined the french windows thoughtfully, constable Lynch said: 'Wasn't there a big deckchair on the beach where all them people disappeared?'

'Think this is the same one do you?'

'Well nobody's around here or next door. Pretty suspicious.'

Lynch came over to me, took out his notebook and tapped my wood. He whispered: 'Are you from round here?'

'Stop talking to the chair Lynch. We've got a mystery to sort out.'

'But Sarge – that deckchair looks guilty.'

'You need a holiday.'

'You don't think it's a bit of a coincidence? Can't be many 30-foot-high deckchairs in the world.'

I was so nervous that I accidentally belched.

'Sarge!!!!'

'What?'

'It......it burped!'

'Don't blame the chair lad.'

'It's got indigestion from eating people.'

'Lynch! Pull yourself together. It's just a big chair. Whoever lives here is probably a friggin' artist or something.'

The young constable quailed and went into the house. A minute later he shrieked!

'What is it?' asked the sergeant running inside. 'A body?'

'No. These little chairs.'

'Will you shut up about bleedin' chairs!'

'But can't you see? They're a cross between the one out

there and this rocking chair?'

'You've lost your marbles sonny.'

'No. They're breeding! Killer chairs!'

'Okay Lynch. Take it easy. I'm going to radio for help.'

'Good stuff Sarge, we'll need more than us two to tackle that big bastard.'

'Help for you! You idiot. Now sit down.'

'No way! I'm not getting eaten!' he shrieked, and ran from the house and garden, followed by a worried-looking colleague.

That night, the ancient instinct to migrate coursing through me and the family in my looping canvas hem, I flew over the spangly lights of the town. It was a long hard flight. Many chairs don't make it, starve or get blown off course. We hid in art centres during the day, posing as exhibits. At times when I heard the kids pining for a mouthful of food, a mere eyeball or nose, I almost succumbed to biting the head off an arts administrator or toilet cleaner. But I didn't want to leave behind any clues. So I comforted everyone with the thought that soon we'd be chomping big fat holidaymakers fried in Ambre Solaire.

We reached Brighton weary, dirty and in need of varnishing. During the night we stacked ourselves by the pier, and at daybreak, I tried to talk to some of the other chairs, but they were modern, unlike any I'd seen.

'We don't want any dirty rockers on our beach man.'

'Yeah... We're sharp, neat, stylish.'

'Pete Townsend sat on me last week.'

They looked mean as their owner set them out. They shouted threats at us whenever humans were out of earshot. Things might not have turned so nasty if an overweight customer hadn't ripped one of them. As my kids laughed and rocked, the stacked mod chairs that hadn't been hired yet suddenly went over like dominoes and set themselves up.

Humans nearby looked on in puzzlement, as these crazy spiv chairs started to push and shove my kids.

'Get out of it you dirty rockers!'

My kids got ready to brawl. One picked up a bike chain and swung it. Another grew studded leather upholstery. Swimmers stood amazed in the sea, as mod chairs heaved humans onto the sand and clacked aggressively towards us. Holidaymakers scattered screaming as the two groups of chairs went for each other. Donkeys leapt out of the way, and galloped braying down the promenade. We were outnumbered, but I was big enough to gnash twenty mods at a time. They didn't look so neat and stylish after me and the kids had finished with them. I was so absorbed in crunching plastic and tearing canvas that I didn't hear the sirens. I didn't realise the police had hit the scene until I got sprayed by water cannons. They flattened us like a hurricane. I saw mods cartwheeling over the sand, and skidding flat into the waves. Then *I* was hit and folded up. Hundreds of constables leapt on top of me, chaining my struts so I couldn't fly or eat them. I saw Constable Lynch:

'Hold him tight lads. He's a killer. A dangerous bastard.'

I struggled as I was led away for questioning. I saw Chi-chi lying on the ground. She'd been broken to bits in the fight.

After that nothing mattered any more. In a police cell, I confessed everything to Lynch. All I could think of was that I'd ruined my darling Chi-chi's life. The kids visited me during the trial. I knew, as I was a deckchair, it would be a set up. There wasn't a single chair on the jury. My kids though, they were great little chairs. The image of their mum. They'd tried unsuccessfully to glue her together. They put in a plea for clemency when I was found guilty of murdering 131 people. But I was ready to fry. For poor dead Chi-chi's sake, I was ready to go to the electric human.